SILENCE
(Sessizlik)

Short stories by
Engin Akyürek

Flexible Press
Minneapolis, Minnesota 2023

COPYRIGHT © 2023 Flexible Press, LLC
All rights reserved. This book cannot be completely quoted, copied, reproduced, or published without a written permission from the publisher. This is a work of fiction. Names, characters, places, and incidents either are the products of the author's imagination or are used fictitiously, and any resemblance to an actual person, living or dead, is entirely coincidental.

Print ISBN: 979-8-9862459-4-2
eBook ISBN: 979-8-9862459-5-9

Flexible Press LLC
Minneapolis, Minnesota 2022
www.flexiblepub.com

Translated from Turkish by
Doina L. Kovalik and Atiye Erden
Published in English with permission from
Doğan Yayınları Yayıncılık ve Yapımcılık A.Ş.
Cover Design: Feyza Filiz
First published in Turkish, September 2018

To İdil Hafızoğlu, the editor of Kafasina Göre, Yasin Öksüz, Nalan Alaca, Basri Albayrak, Özlem Durak, Ankara, and my dear family. Thank you.

—Engin Akyürek

Engin Akyürek's royalties from this book are donated to the Darüşşafaka Society, which works to create a better future for needy, talented students with one or no parents.

Table of Contents

Foreword i
Publisher's Note v

The Cherry Tree 3
A Breath in the Darkness 17
One Night 25
You Mean, Mellow 33
Silence 43
Hello 51
A Brief Story about Love 59
Bad Luck 67
Misty Eyes 77
The Child in Me 83
The German Shepherd 89
Marbles 95
Hasan, Son of Ahmet 103
With a Smile 109
The Old Woman 113
The Smell 121
The Snowman 127
To Leave 135
Memories in the Air 141
Let's Meet in Stories 149
It's Mellow! 157

About the author 163

Foreword

The intense political discourse during the 2019 US election season and the subsequent outbreak of a violent and little-known disease, which shortly thereafter engulfed the world, caused some people to feel they lived in a maddening world. Many of those people felt the urge to run away and isolate, not only their physical bodies, which they were strongly urged to do, but also their mind. Such people, myself included, just needed a little break from those realities of life. I chose a handy remedy: watching movies—yet not any type of movie, but solely movies with enthusiastic, energetic, optimistic, beautiful young people. In a word, unlike Frost, I chose the "trodden road," in that for many, watching a movie is an escape from reality. For me, that trodden road "has made all the difference."

Among many other movies, I watched *Black Money Love.* I was impressed not only by the skillful way in which modern life and traditions mingle in it, but also by the talented cast. A short search on the Internet, and there he was—Engin Akyürek, the actor who played the main male protagonist. The young actor, I learned, was an author as well. He had published a collection of short stories entitled *Sessizlik* (*Silence*) in his native Turkey a few years prior. Now I was curious. I continued my research and discovered that the collection had been enthusiastically received by the public, and it had been translated into many languages.

My co-translator, Atiye Erden, and I were granted permission to translate the collection into English. We embarked upon the translation, animated by the desire to share Akyürek's stories with an American readership eager to embrace novel cultural perspectives, presented in the fiction of an emerging author who had created his work in a language other than English.

Silence consists of twenty-one short stories in which silence proves to mean many a thing in addition to the absence of speech or avoidance to address something or someone. Silence can mean simplicity, harmony, dimmed sense of time, end of a relationship, a newfound love, stillness, reticence, as well as an inner refuge from—to again use the Thomas Hardy phrase already alluded to—the "madding crowd." The stories are captivating, and they stay with the reader long after one exits the sphere of fiction. The stories are deemed "deep and poignant" and "a great read" by Amazon customers who have read the Turkish version. The associative imagery is surprising, and past events are portrayed vividly. The language is carefully crafted, and according to a fan of the e-book in Turkey, "Such a fluent language arouses curiosity."

And there is the past, a past so much alive. Akyürek seems to agree with—nay, build upon—Faulkner's famous line, "The past is never dead. It is not even past."

For many among us, past experiences represent a ubiquity in the silent reality of our minds and souls.

My co-translator and I do hope the experience of reading Akyürek's short stories will be stored in the silence of your soul.

—Doina L. Kovalik, translator

Publisher's Note

I, being your typical American, had not heard of Engin Akyürek until I was approached by Doina L. Kovalik. Kovalik and her colleague Atiye Erden had translated his short story collection and now wanted to find a US publisher. Kovalik described Engin Akyürek as an actor highly acclaimed in his country as well as abroad.

I was intrigued. Adding interest to the project was that Akyürek would donate his royalties to the Darüşşafaka Society in Turkey, which works to create a better future for needy, talented students with one or no parents. At the same time, translators Kovalik and Erden wanted their royalties to go to a worthy cause as well, one that would help increase understanding between Turkish and American cultures.

Supporting various causes is part of Flexible Press's DNA. But for everything we publish, the writing comes first.

I read *Silence* and was delighted. Here was a snapshot of not only a different culture, but a different time. One of children making their own world. One of generations of family together, woven into each other's lives. One of change, showing pre-21st century, pre-cellphone, maybe even pre-complications of the modern world.

I set out to learn more about this big-name TV and movie star in Turkey.

I found out that Akyürek was born in 1981 in Ankara, his father a government official and his mother a homemaker. In 2002, he graduated from Ankara University with a degree in history.

At the same time, Akyürek was interested and involved in theater. He got his big break in show business in 2004 when he won the *Türkiye'nin Yildizlari (Turkey's Star)* TV competition. This led to a supporting role in the TV series, *Yabanci Damat (Foreign Groom)* (2004–2007), where he appeared in all 106 episodes. His film debut was in Zeki Demirkubuz's *Kader (Destiny)* (2006). For his portrayal of Cevat in this film, Akyürek received the Most Promising Actor award for both the Turkish Cinema Awards and the Cagdas Sinema Oyuncuları Dernegi Awards.

He was just getting started. At the time I'm writing this, he has appeared in five films, starring in four, and nine TV series, starring in six. Akyürek returned to the small screen in 2019 with his series *Sefirin Kızı* (*The Ambassador's Daughter*) and in 2022 with the Disney+ series *Kaçis*. In addition, Akyürek is no stranger to theater, having starred in the 2007 play *Romantika Muzikal* (*Romance Musical*).

Throughout his career, Akyürek has had a love of writing. He continues to express himself by writing short stories, having found a home with the *Kafasına Göre* literary magazine. (Where he finds the time, considering how successful and prolific his acting career is, is, to me, a mystery.)

His writing eventually culminated in the publication of this collection in Turkish in 2018. Now, thanks to the hard work and persistence of the translators Kovalik and Erden, we are excited to make this book available in English.

Thank you, Kovalik, for approaching us with this opportunity and helping maneuver the project through a variety of international hurdles.

Thank you, Özgür Emir and Dogan Yayinlari Yayincilik Ve Yapimcilik A.S., the original Turkish publisher, for supporting this project and making it possible.

We are proud to support Akyürek's writing and to play a part in bringing Engin Akyürek to a wider audience. We are also proud that US royalties from this book are going to the Aziz and Gwen Sancar Foundation and the Sancar Turkish Cultural and Community Center in Chapel Hill, North Carolina, a nonprofit organization dedicated to increasing understanding of Turkey and its people, customs, and history.

—*William E Burleson, publisher,*
Flexible Press LLC
Minneapolis, Minnesota, USA

SILENCE

The Cherry Tree

I was in the top of the cherry tree...

The yard and the cherry tree of grumpy old Uncle Hüseyin were like a fresh oil painting. You wouldn't see those roses, the flowers, and the trees anywhere else. Uncle Hüseyin would take care of his yard with the meticulousness of a botanist. He was a retired park keeper, so he had knowledge of plants and fertilizers. The main praise would always go to the cherry tree, even though the beauty of the apricot tree and the greatness of the mulberry tree would build a bridge between your eyes and stomach.

Uncle Hüseyin and his wife had probably fallen asleep already. The couple would turn off the lights soon after sunset. As soon as the lights went off, we, the neighborhood's usual pranksters, jumped over the wired fence and entered the yard. Hakan was the lookout, Mehmet climbed the apricot tree, Selim and I stretched out on the deepest branches of the cherry tree. I was on the tree's highest branch, and I was enjoying it as if I had climbed the Himalayas. The cupboard at home was full of fruit, but I found it very organic to climb the tree to eat the fruit.

I was experiencing an adrenaline rush with mixed emotions of success and proscription. We neither carried bag nor stuffed our pockets; we were only eating what we found. We were as greedy as our little stomachs allowed. We crammed Hakan's share into our pockets, curbing our appetite so we wouldn't upset our stomachs. There were some details we had to keep in mind. For example, we never left the pits around the tree. If Uncle Hüseyin found the pits in the morning, he would split us up into atoms before noontime prayer. Nonetheless, it would have felt so good to spit the pits into the air, given that delicious sweet and slightly sour taste in our mouths. But we couldn't have the cake and eat it too.

Hakan's high-pitched voice pierced our ears.

Hakan was scared. With his sense of duty, he let his panic loose, which was stuck between his heart and his voice. The gate's bell started ringing. Hakan had already climbed the fence and left. I never thought the iron gate was going to open. Uncle Hüseyin should have been asleep already. The bell was ringing persistently. I waited motionless in the top of the tree. Who in

SILENCE

their right mind would disturb Uncle Hüseyin and his wife at this hour?

Just as the iron gate's pathetic ringing noise ceased, there followed the even more pathetic noise of the gate opening. Ah, Uncle Hüseyin, was that really necessary now?

Mehmet and Selim climbed down and disappeared into the darkness as soon as they heard the gate open. The shadows of the two heads created a scary scene. I had no choice but to hide in the tree.

There came a loud noise created by silence. My teenage heart was fluttering in my mouth together with the noises created by the movement of the shadows along the pathway. The shadows of the two heads had become joined to the bodies.

I could see my mom and dad from atop the tree. It was the fourth day of the Eid, and my parents had wished to finish their Eid visits, even though it was late in the day.

My arms and legs had melted into the limbs of the cherry tree. I waited in silence as if I had become part of the tree. I was about to go through photosynthesis and evaporate when Uncle Hüseyin's wife opened the iron gate to let my parents in.

Uncle Hüseyin's wife opened the door of the house. Just as my parents were about to remove their shoes to enter, Uncle Hüseyin's voice snuck out of the house and into the yard.

"Let's sit outside. The weather is beautiful."

The table, the chairs, and the tea set were all moved under the cherry tree. The tree was lit up with lights; Uncle Hüseyin's design. I was as visible as an amusement park mascot. They would have seen me, had they looked up and wished one another "Happy Eid." The sentences that started with "Happy Eid" were followed by many similar ones. The tea glasses were filled as soon as they became empty.

My waiting in the tree became quite tiresome. I had to pee. I wanted to unzip my pants and let it go. Uncle Hüseyin's bald head was my target. I was afraid the gentle breeze would change the trajectory of the jet, so I decided to wait. But the pain in my groin became more and more acute, and suddenly I fell down, together with the branch I perched on. I fell at my parents' feet, near Uncle Hüseyin: "Happy Eid..."

My eyes were overwhelmed by the dark. There was a new color created by the darkness. The various blacks caused rainbow rings to come into being, pulling me in.

I was in bed when I opened my eyes. I wasn't feeling the pain that should have come from the soft tissues of my body. A mothball smell burned my throat. Where was I? What was I doing in this room? Judging by the old furniture, I wasn't in a hospital room. I tried to get out of bed but fell onto the floor. There was an unusual imbalance and disproportion in my young body.

When I saw my reflection in the mirror as I was walking toward the window, I knew I was having a nightmare. The nightmare was hiding in a fifteen-year-old's subconscious. My youthful body had turned into a fifty-year-old one. My voice had changed, my hair had fallen; I found myself in the body of a man I didn't know. As I inspected my face in the mirror, I thought to myself it would be away by the time I woke up. When I hit my head during the fall, some doors must have opened in my brain that shouldn't have. Maybe I should enjoy this. I was having a nightmare, but maybe I was in control. I should enjoy this until I woke up. After all, it was a nightmare.

The depth of my voice rang like a childish melody in my ears. At that very moment, a woman about the same age as the man whose body I was in came into the room.

The details of my nightmare were becoming scary. Each was so scary that I even figured out the brand of the doorknob. The woman had obviously been living in this room for a long time. She quickly changed the sheets. She was arranging things in the closet as efficiently as a ten-finger typist. I turned my back while she changed her clothes. I knew this was a nightmare, but the room still wasn't mine. I said to myself we were married when she repeated her question.

"Are you ready, Bey?"

I was standing in front of the mirror. I meant to say this was a nightmare, but no sound came out. She approached me with smiling eyes and graciously put her hand on my head.

"Are you okay? You're not running a fever."

"I'm fine."

"You need to get ready."

"For what?"

The words coming out of my mouth were as heavy as my body. There was silence every time I tried to state this was a nightmare. Whoever was in charge of my nightmare was censoring that sentence.

"What do you mean, for what? Have you forgotten? They are coming over to ask for our daughter's hand in marriage."

Well, I might as well have a daughter since I was married. It was only normal that she be of marriageable age, given that I was old.

I couldn't remember when I had put on the suit that my wife had placed on the bed for me. Clearly, it was a suit for special occasions. I was a family man, but I didn't know how many kids I

SILENCE

had or how old I was. I felt like I had been placed on a stage when I came out of the bedroom. I was walking very carefully. The squeaky noise made by the wooden floor was annoying. There was food on the table in the living room. A young girl came out of the kitchen, holding a tray. She put the tray on the table, ran to me, and gave me a hug.

"Daddy, dear!"

Doubtless, she took after her mother. The guy whose body I was in did not have any nice features on his face. I tried to smile, but the guy's face muscles, which hadn't worked in years, merely managed to produce a half-smile.

I hastily sat on a chair by the table, trying not to mess up my suit. My daughter was beautiful. She definitely didn't take after me. I wondered if the groom-to-be deserved her. The door next to the kitchen opened, and a teenage boy came out. I could tell who he took after. He had an acne-suffering adolescent's face, less comely than my daughter's and my wife's. He had obviously just woken up. He went into the bathroom, scratching his head. He didn't even bother to say good morning to me or give me a hug.

I started feeling bored. I wanted to get out of the suit, go back to bed, and rid myself of the nightmare. There was a china cabinet in front of me, made of walnut. I was familiar with walnut trees. There used to be one in Uncle Hüseyin's yard; he had to cut it down when it got infested with insects. There was a newspaper on one of the shelves in the china cabinet. I saw the year of publication: 1940. I wondered what I was doing in a picture that I had never seen before. It would have been more fun and technologically advanced if I had faced a nightmare one hundred years from now. I could have brought back some stuff to the present in my dreams.

My nightmare wife was dressed smartly. She didn't know what to do with her anxiety while dusting with one hand, ironing the teenage boy's clothes with the other, and bringing the food in from the kitchen. I was watching my little family and getting used to this house and its mothball smell.

The doorbell rang with a bird-sounding chime, similar to the one we had at my house. I knew I had to be calm in my capacity as a father. The groom-to-be and his family came in quite noisily but humbly. The groom-to-be looked like he was in his twenties. I could tell he was going to be bald like me. His parents appeared to be reasonable people. They just didn't know what to say. I watched the groom-to-be as they sat down. I might have been young, but I had the brains and intuition to read people. The coffee came after the introductory conversation. My beautiful daughter had made it. It was the first time ever in my fifteen years that I had Turkish coffee.

The mother of the groom-to-be was talking too much, using sentences whose meanings I didn't get. My eyes were on the groom-to-be; his behavior was not reassuring to me. He also watched me every now and then, casting a timid look. The father of the groom-to-be finally brought up the issue of asking for my daughter's hand in marriage. I was the father, and the final decision was mine. My daughter looked me in the eye like a baby gazelle, waiting for me to say yes. I didn't like the groom-to-be. He didn't have a trustworthy demeanor. He avoided looking at me.

My beautiful daughter cleared the empty coffee cups and laid the cake and the box of chocolates, brought by the groom's family, on the crate that was being used as a coffee table. This was the best part of the nightmare. The coffee and pastries were not enough for me. I pulled the coffee table near myself and started shoving everything into my mouth. The role of the father was over; this was my nightmare! I finished the box of chocolates under my family's condemning stare. The chocolates tasted like locust beans rather than cocoa. My lips and teeth were syrupy. Everybody was staring at me. I excused myself and tried to make for the bathroom, even though I didn't know where it was.

The groom-to-be stuck his head in the bathroom while I was rinsing my mouth. I could see him in the mirror without turning my head. The excitement in his eyes had gotten stronger; he looked like he wanted to tell me something.

He came in, looked around suspiciously, and closed the bathroom door.

"Hey, didn't you recognize me?"

How dare he talk to his future father-in-law like that.

"What are you saying, son?"

"Come on, stop 'sonning' me!"

"What's up?"

"Didn't you recognize me?"

"Noo..."

"Hakan, I'm Hakan..."

"Hakan? Hakan who?"

"How many Hakans do you know?"

What was Hakan doing in my nightmare? He had fled without looking back.

"You filthy deserter! What are you doing here?"

"I didn't come here of my own accord."

I moved closer to him, took a good look at him, and to my surprise, I noticed his teenage self in his eyes. Using a fatherly voice, I said, "This is my nightmare. What are you doing in it?"

SILENCE

"What do you mean, your nightmare? It's my nightmare!"

I was in a bathroom with my future son-in-law, arguing about nightmares!

"You deserter. You jumped over the fence and ran away. I fell out of the cherry tree right onto my head and ended up here."

"As if I didn't..."

"What?"

"I fell as I was jumping over the fence. When I opened my eyes, I was in this ugly body of a soon-to-be bridegroom. I tried my best to explain and escape for hours on end, but to no avail..."

"What are you saying?" I asked. "Won't we ever be out of this?"

"I don't know," Hakan replied. "I tried to go back to sleep, but I didn't get any."

I quivered as if the guy whose body I was in had my soul too.

I was in a huge body. It should have been impossible for him to recognize me.

"I could..."

"How come I didn't recognize you?"

"You see me from a fatherly perspective."

"Shut up, deserter. You wanna marry my daughter now?"

"What say you? Marry? And how come she's your daughter?"

"Well, you'll see when I tell everybody in there . . ."

"You are mean . . . and dishonest! You are just as mean as the guy you're impersonating."

My wife politely knocked on the door.

"Are you in there, Bey?"

"I'm coming, ma'am."

Hakan and I looked at each other and started laughing while exchanging friendly punches.

"Bey. . ."

Hakan went back into his new character as he left the bathroom.

"You have a beautiful daughter."

I exited the bathroom and returned to my role as a father. I knew Hakan, and it was no coincidence that he was in this guy's body. I wasn't going to let this guy marry my daughter. Taking my time, I carefully looked at the groom's father, my wife, and everyone else in the living room. The possibility was there that people I knew and didn't like were in these bodies. I distrusted that big adolescent son of mine.

The groom's father had come to the end of his speech and requested that I allow my daughter to marry his son, God willing. Silence followed, and everybody waited for me to speak. I pulled the

SILENCE

coffee table in front of me even closer and started eating the cake. My silence granted my answer more weight. Every person in the living room was waiting politely for my answer.

"I don't think this marriage. . ."

I blacked out before I finished my sentence. I fainted and slid off the chair onto the floor. My eyes were at the same level as the cake on the coffee table. Everybody was around me, and voices were coming from all over.

I was in the emergency room when I opened my eyes. My mom and dad were looking at me in panic.

"Are you okay, son?" my mom asked.

"I'm okay, Mom."

My head was bandaged; I had wounds to my mouth and eyes. My dad was caressing my head; obviously he had forgotten about the cherry-stealing incident.

"Uncle Hüseyin sent you some cherries. Would you care for some?"

As I was trying to find something to say, I heard Hakan's voice from behind the curtains.

"Aah. . ."

My mom saw the confusion on my face.

"Yes, Hakan fell on his head when jumping off the fence. God bless. . ."

I turned my head and saw Hakan through the curtains. His head was getting stitched. The curtains were moving as the doctor moved, allowing us to see each other. While the doctor was finishing up, Hakan whispered as if he knew everything:

"Don't you dare eat those cherries!"

I closed my eyes and buried my head in my pillow. I noticed a taste in my mouth: cherries.

A Breath in the Darkness

Hakan called me, near breathless and with a mourning voice.

"My grandpa has passed away."

Uncle İsmet, Hakan's grandpa, had been my childhood mentor. He had lost his sight after a high fever disease during his childhood. Yet he had found the colors to brighten up his long ninety-year existence. He never minded his blindness. He, a three-pack-a-day smoker, would take another puff and change the subject when the conversation turned to his blindness. He was quite young looking in comparison to his peers. He always wore a shirt and tie, a rule exacted by his wife, Hatice. If you asked around, his friends and neighbors would refer to him as a carefree individual with a permanent, half-moon-shaped smile who wouldn't take anything seriously. Nobody had ever asked me about him, but if they had, I would have had a lot to say: that he would smile with his blind eyes and readily invite you to his inner amusement park; that he showed leniency to the mischief Hakan and I caused by gently caressing our heads.

His smoking was like a state-of-the-art performance staged by a fine craftsman. I would have loved for you to have seen the way he held his cigarette, put it between his lips, lit it and took a breath in from it, and exhaled the smoke as if he were reading a love poem. His children had constantly tried to make him quit, but he would always take a drag on his cigarette and say, "I'm not gonna live forever anyway." He never lost his smile or his way. He would walk by taking small steps and would find his way wherever he was going without anyone's help. He developed a humpback after his wife passed away. It was a hump caused by loneliness. Losing your life partner and your lifelong guide wasn't easy.

He would take all the kids in the neighborhood to the Republic Day and National Children's Day festivities in Ankara's May 19th Stadium. We would get into several taxis and celebrate the holidays by chasing each other, honking horns, and flying flags. "Holidays should feel like holidays" was Uncle İsmet's motto.

It was the first day of the Eid, and the entire house had undergone "Mom's cleaning." You could eat off the floor. The new outfits had been unwrapped, all those around had a smile on their faces, and the coffee table was placed strategically. The chocolates were on standby, the candy was ready for the kids, and everybody who rang the doorbell would get splashed with lemon cologne.

Uncle İsmet loved my dad and would always drop by on the first day of the Eid. There were unwritten rules to show love and respect: One's first-day visits were more valuable than one's last-day visits, which were considered return visits. I served Uncle İsmet chocolates and received my monetary gift from him. He was usually the speaker, whatever the subject was. I always enjoyed listening to him and would laugh out loud. But sometimes I had to hold my laughs back because my dad would look at me and raise his eyebrows, a signal to me to be quiet. But if an old man's stories brought laughter to a child, it meant there was a lot left to laugh about in the world.

Uncle İsmet had put out his cigarette and was searching for another one in his jacket's inner pocket. He realized his pack was empty. My dad offered him a cigarette from the packs on the coffee table.

Before even putting it between his lips, Uncle İsmet said, "I can't smoke this; 'tis not my brand."

People didn't go to balconies to smoke in those days; everybody smoked inside.

"I'll go get you some, Uncle İsmet."

"I don't want to be a burden."

The coffee had not been served yet, and the stories to be told were just being considered. I put the money for the cigarettes in my pocket and ran to the store. I was going to be back before they had a chance to drink their coffee.

It was a holiday, and the neighborhood market was closed. It was about to get dark. I ran to the next neighborhood market and was breathless when I saw the "closed" sign. I was either going to give up or continue to look for an open store. A child's feeling of responsibility was selfless, heartfelt, and conscientious, contrary to what he learns later in life.

I couldn't return home empty-handed. I was running and looking for an open store in the darkness. I was far from home. At this point, I would to be able to get his cigarettes only if he stayed at my place overnight. My short legs made me miscalculate the distance perhaps, but I think I was three or four kilometers away from home. My new outfit was all dusty and messy. My feet ached. I could hear my breath and feel my sweaty neck and armpits with every step.

I was about to give up and return home when I saw the neon sign of a store between two buildings. I caught my breath and entered the store. My only fear was that the store would be out of Uncle Ismet's cigarette brand. The store owner searched the shelf and found a pack. The money in my hand was damp with sweat, and my clothes were messy. So my appearance was a little sketchy.

The man handed me the pack of cigarettes and said, "You're not going to smoke, are you?"

I didn't know what to say, for I hadn't expected that question. "And a box of matches," I said as he gave me the change.

Just what did he think I was going to do? That I was going to smoke Uncle İsmet's cigarettes? I felt the adrenaline caused by the guilt. I quickly left the store and found a quiet place. For the first time in my life, I was going to smoke. I opened the pack at the wrong end, hoping I could make it look like it had never been opened. I put the cigarette between my lips and lit it. It felt like somebody had stuffed a bunch of dried grass and hay in my mouth and set it afire. I started coughing, and tears were running down my face. I threw the cigarette away before my hands and face stank of smoke.

I didn't have a watch, but I knew how far I was from my house. I breathed into my palms to measure the nicotine level in my breath while also thinking about how I was going to make the pack look intact.

As I got close to home, I could see my parents and neighbors running around. The echo of my name in the silent night was eerie.

Everybody in the neighborhood was looking for me. I hid behind a light pole, trying to figure out what to do. It was much later than I had expected. The tear in the cigarette pack had gotten bigger, and my feeling of guilt kept me in hiding.

I observed the people. I noticed the fear in my mother's eyes and the neighbors' efforts to comfort her. Hakan looked like he had just woken up and was trying to figure out what was happening. Everything was real. Those were real emotions that even famous actors couldn't render—and the best directors couldn't convey. Watching such a reality affected my young body. There had to be a limit to it. I felt like I was watching people I knew in their bedrooms, meddling in their private lives.

My mother got even more alarmed when the police arrived. I was scared. The police car's red light turned my face red, reflecting my inner world.

The shadows passing by me looked very scary. It was getting cold. The frosty weather of Ankara was showing its teeth. I was sitting behind the pole, leaning my head against it; I was tired. I saw a shadow on the pole and felt a hand touch my

SILENCE

shoulder. As I turned my head, I heard Uncle Ismet's soft, comforting voice.

"You naughty boy."

I didn't know what to say. I was surprised that of all those people, he was the one who found me in the dark.

"Here, Uncle İsmet. Your cigarettes."

He put the pack in his pocket and held the back of my neck with his warm hand.

"Let's go home."

A deep silence engulfed the street as we walked home, with everybody surprised that he'd found me. He was walking like a hero. He gently squeezed my neck and, in a low voice, said, "Don't you ever smoke again, okay?"

I remained silent. Every word I'd meant to say had vanished into the darkness. I have never smoked again, thus having kept the promise I silently made that day.

Hakan called me, near breathless and with a mourning voice.

"My grandpa has passed away."

As I hung up the phone, my memories of Uncle İsmet went roaming around the room, blending into the cool air coming in from the open window and caressing my face like his voice. I had a little smile on my face and a toothpick between my lips. I was aware of no recipes or formulas for recollections.

I closed my eyes and took in a breath in the darkness around me...

One Night

I recognized her laugh. My ex-girlfriend was sitting at the table across the room. She hadn't seen me; she wouldn't have smiled or laughed if she had. We were in an upscale restaurant. The seriousness inside was worthy of people who could afford to pay a hefty check. I needed to be careful about my stares because I was with my new girlfriend, and she could have instinctively noticed them. I felt like I was taking an exam on a subject I wasn't knowledgeable about. God forbid, the calm and confident male profile I had displayed up until now might be ruined. Situations similar to this one were highly common in the modern world, but at that moment and at that table, I felt primitive.

When she quieted her laugh, the shields created by her laughter vanished, and the guy she was with surfaced. They both had rings on their fingers, and they were comfortably sitting and smiling. The guy was like a reference point between my past and my future. I would have laughed at myself had I used a sentence like that before. I didn't know what was happening. I had a new girlfriend, and I was happy, no question about that.

Everything would have been okay, with everything staying in the past, if I had listened to my gut feeling, asked for the check, and left. But an irrational feeling, a sense of curiosity, had captured my body. My mind was telling me to leave and put an end to this, but I refused to listen.

I knew my fake smile wasn't convincing. Just like a killer's return to the crime scene, my stupid smile was showing off my guilt. Was there an unfinished love story involving anything left unsaid? Sometimes you can't control your feelings. Pictures and words I didn't know existed came to mind out of nowhere. There were sentences I wouldn't dare to read and pictures I wouldn't enjoy.

My face was as red as a young boy's. My girlfriend must have sensed my anxiousness.

"Are you okay, darling?"

"I'm fine."

"Hmm . . . You normally don't eat this fast."

"I've been hungry."

SILENCE

I didn't realize I had been eating fast. If you had asked me, I would have said I had only had a glass of water and a bite of meat.

I glanced at my ex-girlfriend. She was also eating meat. She liked her meat well-done, yet she normally preferred vegetables. Her preference for meat meant she had gotten up early, had exercised, and had had a busy day. Three years later, she was still not a vegan; obviously she'd postponed some things. Time could change some things, but not all. Her way of cutting the meat into pieces felt like she was cutting my body, and my heart was softening as she chewed. I decided to go on with the mundane conversation with my girlfriend.

"The meat is good."

"Are you okay?"

"Would you like a piece of meat?"

"You know I don't eat meat."

Actually, I didn't know anything. I had forgotten everything I knew. I realized some things were not going to be the same anymore. If I hadn't seen my ex, perhaps life would have eliminated some inviting questions. Perhaps life would have waited for the next trial. There was no need for life to ask me questions. The answers to the questions I couldn't ask myself were at that table. I wasn't sure whether I was happy, but my ex's happiness was making me feel like I should be unhappy. How could a human being at times be like a damp and rusty piece of metal bought from a scrap dealer?

She couldn't not have seen me. I was right in front of her. The difference was that she knew how to control her feelings. Given her feminine intuition, she knew how to transpose the two-table-length distance into a very far-off one.

Before we ordered the dessert, she walked in slow motion past the table toward the bathroom. I felt a breeze in my face, as if she had touched my hair. I had just taken a sip of water, and my lips were still wet. That looked like drool in the overhead light. I started gulping down my drink as if I had just found water in the desert.

Lightly drying my mouth with a napkin, I got up from the table and started walking. What? Was I about to follow her to the bathroom? I started questioning my morality. I had done the first thing that occurred to me, and I pretended to be talking on the phone before reaching the bathroom. I looked extremely kinky and stupid.

It was hard to pretend to be talking on the phone. The waiters walking past me smiled as if they knew I was faking it. Sometimes I pretended I was listening and with a serious face made "hm-hm, hm-hm" replies.

The sound of her high heels prompted nervousness in me. I turned my whole body toward her. She couldn't avoid me. Our eyes met. For about a quarter of a second, we stood silently. She acted like she didn't want time to stop, like she didn't want to create another memory. I realized she wanted to leave, yet she was unable to move. She didn't know what to do with her hands, and she straightened her hair. I might be telling this in great lengths, yet the whole thing happened in a fraction of a second. She walked past me like a breeze. As she walked toward her table, her footsteps echoed in my brain.

I went outside. I needed some fresh air. I wanted the fresh air to demolish my stupidity. I wanted to hide somewhere. A valet was enjoying a cigarette right in front of me. I felt like beating him up. Sometimes things that trigger anger might be tragic and comical at the same time.

"Mind if I bum a cigarette?"

"Sure, sir."

He took a cigarette from the pack, put it in his mouth, and lit it with his own cigarette. Then he attempted to wipe my cigarette with his fingertips before handing it to me.

"Hope that's not disgusting to you."

"No worries."

I was going to smoke and go inside before I got too cold. It had just started to snow. The cars looked like they were covered with powdered sugar. Such a view befitted a night like this.

"Could I have a cigarette too?"

"Yes, ma'am."

She had followed me outside. I took the cigarette from the valet before he had a chance to put it in his mouth and light it. I put it between my lips and lit it with my cigarette. I did not want the valet to ask her the same question. My ex, the valet, and I smoked without talking. All the smoke we exhaled created a funny graphic.

She looked at her lipstick-stained cigarette and said, "You started smoking?"

"It's my first smoke ever. How about you?" Cough. "Do you smoke?" Cough.

"My first smoke as well." Cough.

We both coughed, yet on different pitches. I didn't want to finish my cigarette and even considered asking for another one. The valet didn't cough. He inhaled and exhaled the smoke between his yellow teeth with ease. My ex-girlfriend and I looked into each other's eyes and exhaled the smoke simultaneously as if we were kissing.

"Twenty-eight's coming."

The valet's yell disturbed that smoky atmosphere, and she ran inside. I could have beaten the heck out of him. The reason behind my anger wouldn't possibly have passed unnoticed. I would have gotten a reduced sentence.

SILENCE

My phone rang. I realized that I had five missed calls from my current girlfriend. I went in and headed for my table. All of a sudden, an indescribable expression appeared on my face. My ex, her fiancé, and my girlfriend were sitting at our table. Unlike visual receptors, the brain is unable to react instantly under such circumstances.

What could they be doing? I anxiously walked toward the table. My girlfriend stood up when she saw me.

"Honey, come here. Meet my friend from college, Umit. I haven't seen him for a long time. And this is his fiancée—sorry, what did you say your name was?"

"Hello!"

"They're getting married this weekend. We'll attend, won't we, honey?"

Cough. "We will. . ."

You Mean, Mellow

He was staring at me shamelessly.

That attitude had nothing to do with the length of our relationship. When such was the case, he would stare at me, mocking me and failing to fulfill his duties. You know, even cats have duties. They are supposed to let you pet them, to purr and meow at you, to create a guilty feeling in you even though it be for fun. Those are the kind of things I mean.

Every relationship can be summarized in one sentence. The summary of our relationship was a cat.

I remember the day the cat—I mean, our cat—first came to my house. How could I have forgotten? It was during the second week of our relationship, the very day she moved in with me. My girlfriend came over with her suitcase, her toothbrush, and her newly adopted kitten, adding a new dimension to our relationship. Girlfriends would do such things sometimes, as would cats, leaving their scent all around.

His feline instincts kicked in the moment he first saw me. He purred and somersaulted with joy. He put on a one-act show that he would never perform again.

"What's the cat's name, love?"

"I wanted to name him together."

There was quite a set of names to pick from since the cat was a tabby.

"So what should his name be?"

My tendency to wait things out came to the fore, the way it always does.

"I think we should wait and see his character. Then we'll name him accordingly."

"I think it should be Walnut."

"Walnut? What kind of name is Walnut for a cat?"

"You know, because I like walnuts."

A cat had entered my house, had rubbed up against my furniture, my books. We started off naming him together, and I ended up with a name imposed on him like a ready-made text. Besides, I don't like walnuts; they give me cold sores. Walnut here, Walnut there, we now had a three-person life. As soon as his character came forth, as soon as I saw his happy-go-lucky personality, I realized Walnut was not the right name for him.

SILENCE

"Walnut, come here sweetheart."

"Purr..."

His existence was built upon consuming as little energy as possible, wasting time, and taking nobody seriously. Was this his nature, or was he like this with only me? When he first came to my house, I had thought that he would like me, that he would add some color to the house.

"I think his name should be Mellow, sweetheart."

"Excuse me?"

"It should be Mellow."

"Mellow? Who would call their cat Mellow?"

It was the best name for him. Besides, if a cat could be called Walnut, he could certainly be called Mellow. I didn't want to be one of those parents who would choose bizarre names for their kids. Mellow was a name he could take pride in. The name suited his soul, his tail, as well as his paws. When I called him Mellow, he would glance my way, then he would show me his little tabby behind and walk away as if saying, "See you later."

Meanwhile, my relationship with my girlfriend kept brewing, leaving a weird taste in my mouth. Mellow witnessed all that and, staring at us with his blue eyes, awaited the end of the story. I became a guest in my own house—and Mellow, a landlord. My chair, my bed, basically every corner of the house was his. I had to plead with him to move aside so I might have some space to live.

My relationship with my girlfriend had soured like an overbrewed tea drunk after a bad dinner.

"Walnut!"

"Mellow!"

"Walnut!"

I won't tell you about our fights because they weren't over Walnut or Mellow. We were going through the overtime of a dying relationship. We had found ways to hurt each other and created a senseless ruckus.

"Walnut!"

"Mellow!"

Every relationship is doomed to end; so was ours. She moved out, suitcase and toothbrush and all. Mellow was left purring behind the closed door though.

"Purr..."

I sent word to my girlfriend's, I mean, my ex-girlfriend's friends and relatives and asked her to take Mellow back. She neither came back for him nor sent word. Mellow seemed to smile smugly with his sparkly blue eyes.

"What are you laughing at?"

"Purr..."

SILENCE

The house had gone quiet, with me feeling ever more like a guest at Mellow's place. We had now been together for six months; however, our relationship had never gone beyond my giving him his food and water.

"Don't you love me?"

"Purr..."

"All right, all right."

"Purr..."

He was still looking at me shamelessly. The typical silence following the end of a relationship was disturbed by the annoying noise of Mellow's paws on the parquet floor. He was a reminder of my relationship with her. I would recall the fights between us when giving Mellow his food; I would recall our happy days together when Mellow chewed on my books.

I waited three whole months. I don't know if Mellow did too. He slept well during the nights, while I couldn't. He licked his paws clean as I sat there worrying, purred when I wanted to talk. Time went by, and the household was run such as to please him.

One night, when I felt like I was suffocating, I put Mellow in the car and drove him to a different neighborhood where he would be able to live in peace. I had fed him, taken care of him, given him his name. What more could I have done? I had considered giving him to friends or acquaintances, but his closeness—and his very name—would have brought back memories and opened up old wounds that I was trying to forget. It was best not to know where he was.

I got back home late that night, showered, relaxed, and threw myself onto the bed, intending to start my new life with a good sleep. Something woke me up in the middle of my deep sleep as if something was being whispered in my ear. I quickly got dressed and headed out. The whisper was my own voice. It had travelled down my ear, settled in the space between my heart and stomach, and found new friends there. The words kept screaming that I had never loved Mellow; I had only pretended to. Then they went further and yelled that I had taken up the role of a cat-loving man only because my girlfriend had wanted it. They had been talking to me here and there ever since I could recall, and they had always spoken the truth. It was true that I did not love Mellow; I had only pretended to. Nonetheless, I had meant for him to love me. There was no need for lengthy explanations. Sometimes a cat can make us discover things about life.

I went back to the street where I had left Mellow. I got out of the car and walked toward the place where I had left him. The possibility was there that I might not be able to find him. He wasn't used to being on the streets, and stray dogs posed quite an issue for him. The more I thought about it, the wilder my conscience got, beating me up. I saw him over by the large trash cans; he seemed comfortable, purring with an arrogant "what-took-you-so long" expression on his face.

His face displayed the shine of a wise man who had seen everything life had to offer. He had known I would come back for him and understood that I hadn't liked him when we first met. I, however, had understood nothing and had thrown life out of bounds by means of short passes.

Something changed after we got back home. I got used to being with Mellow, who advanced from the status of guest and settled back into my old room. We made a deal by means of our eyes. We now loved each other rather than merely pretending to. Mellow grew, his round rump becoming larger than his head. He had gotten to a point where he lived up to his name more than ever.

I forgot about my relationship with my ex and grew attached to Mellow. Life was more colorful now. The voices in my mind had grown quieter— and Mellow, fatter. I was in a good mood and felt no need to hold my laughter back. It was as if someone had bestowed colors to all the clouds, streets, and people. Everything was glowing. I think everything had been tinted with a color so I could forget certain things.

Imagine you are having a nice dinner with friends. Your laughter fills the entire place. What would you do if your ex-girlfriend called while you were having the time of your life? Let me tell you: I, for one, would continue laughing, let the phone buzz several times, freeze the laugh on my face, and leave the table, pretending that the call was an unimportant one. I would clear my throat and make sure to make my voice sound distant. Roles change quickly when one is in a good mood and life is good. If your ex-girlfriend is calling you at that hour, it's either because she's in trouble or because she wishes to gibber about how she misses you. Don't mind me; these are ego-filled descriptions that are nothing more than a *mise-en-scène* in defiance of reality.

My hands were sweaty, my voice was cloudy, and not knowing what to say scared me.

"Um, hello."

"Hello. I'm sorry to disturb you at this hour."

"It's all right."

"I'm really sorry. I know we haven't had a chance to talk. I was just wondering how Walnut was doing."

She called me exactly one year later, and she didn't even ask how I was doing; she only remembered her cat, now that things were going well for her.

SILENCE

"Walnut is still with you, right? I've really missed him. Could I stop by and see him sometime? . . . Hello . . . hello . . . Are you there?"

I kept silent, unable to say a single word.

"Hellooo, are you still there?"

I uttered a single sentence as I hung up:

"You mean, Mellow."

Silence

A winter day . . . A cold wind was blowing in Ankara, and it felt like a huge freezer was hanging over the city. The snow had adorned the streets with white embroidery. The rooftops looked like portraits of innocence framed in bridal lace. I was in bed, doing my best not to wake up. I heard voices outside while trying to tuck myself back in. A symphony of weak, unpleasant sounds was audible in the neighborhood. I rested my sleepy head on the steamy window and tried to see what was going on. The father of one of my best friends, Selim, had just passed away. The people in the neighborhood were informing each other about the need of silence of death. I ran out without putting on my coat and my boots but went back in, following my mother's warning, and dressed properly.

The shoes in front of Selim's house displayed the pain in the house. It was obvious that everybody had come quickly. They had put on whatever shoes they'd found; it didn't matter if it was a pair of flip-flops when you were faced with death. I thought, "Oh, Mother! Now they're gonna think I took my time to put on my boots and coat!" I couldn't escape the feeling of "what would people say" even when it was time to mourn.

I rang the doorbell. A little girl opened the door and pointed to the room where Selim was. Her smallness made me sense the reality of death. Selim and the other neighborhood kids were there, trying to lighten the pressure of death by means of keeping silent. Selim's mom and the other old ladies were in the next room, crying and raising laments over his father that nobody could understand. The older men of the neighborhood were in yet another room, looking at the rug on the floor, their heads lowered. Every one of them had a preferred pattern in the rug. Their silent reaction to death materialized in the geometric shapes. I offered my condolences to Selim, and his response was "thank you." There was nothing else to be said. I also put my head down and tried to find a pattern in the rug that suited my inner world.

The tea was served, and all the kids in the neighborhood, myself included, were put to the test of hunger in the face of death. In our childish minds, we wished to withstand death by not eating. We understood each other without raising our heads; however, the growling in our stomachs was too loud. One of the ladies had placed cookies and pastries in front of us. Nobody wanted to be the first to succumb to hunger in a place of mourning. Selim raised his head and said, "Go ahead and eat." Orphan Selim took up the role of father.

I do not remember who made the first move, but I do remember that we ate with a sense of plunder and slapped each other's hands at the same time. When a small child hides inside your body with his little grin, the reality of life suddenly becomes childish. Selim laughed as we were stuffing the pastries in our mouths. He insisted on being a child despite the teachings of psychology and science. Our surprise was short-lived, though, for we all started laughing. The old lady who was serving tea reminded us how to act properly during mourning by saying, "Shh, shame! Your father has just passed away!" As Selim continued laughing, I suggested we go out and get some air. The glow on our faces expressed the triumph of childishness over death. We grabbed our coats and ran outside without saying anything to anybody.

We simply ran without knowing where we were running. We followed Selim, who ran ahead of us up and down the streets. The kids who were wearing flip-flops lagged far behind. We would stop and rest once in a while; we knew we were going to do whatever Selim wanted to that day.

"What are we doing next?" I asked. He looked at me with grieving eyes and started walking in front of us. We first went to an arcade, making some younger kids give up their games so we could play. We allowed Selim to win every game. We even went into a billiard room, despite being underage, courtesy of an older brother of one of the kids. We had no idea what Selim was feeling; for that matter, we were better off not knowing. Once we grew tired of playing with poles taller than ourselves, we started running in the streets. A child approached us and said, "Everybody is asking about you at home, Selim."

Selim made it clear that he wanted to share his pain with us by telling the child, "Okay, you go home now. I'm coming." After all, we were his best friends; we were even closer than some brothers. We walked around the neighborhood and laughed for no reason. It felt good in Ankara's cold weather. Laughs came about as a natural cheering-up tool. Laughter made the snow on the rooftops melt and the flowers bloom. As we walked laughing, the shopkeepers would glance at Selim, saying, "Would a child whose father has just died behave like this?" The shame of humankind, hidden in those glances, revives on every painful or happy occasion.

We ran into Selim's uncle. Upon seeing Selim laugh, he frowned so heavily that the snow on the roofs turned into ice. "Shame on you! What are you doing out here? Your father has just passed away," he said. Selim quietly bowed his head, possibly in search of a rug pattern in the snow.

"I am going home, Uncle."

Our young bodies turned into adult men's bodies at the sound of Selim's quiet but heart-warming voice. It was like Selim was doing his military service, Hakan was married, Veli had children ... We were walking like men! Just as everybody was teaching us how to behave during pain, Selim was teaching us more meaningful things. As soon as his uncle left to deal with the funeral matters, Selim turned to us and said, "Let's not go home." We had agreed to do whatever Selim wanted that day, and I was glad we had.

We found a quiet corner and started to talk rubbish. If you close your eyes and recall a few sentences from your childhood, I'm sure they would convey things quite similar to what Selim was talking about.

When we got hungry, we bought some sodas and chips with the last pocket change we had. We talked about the girls we liked, and we laughed off the fabrications. We did believe Selim, nonetheless, when he talked about the girl he liked. We wanted to believe him. We acquiesced to having been the ones who had lied—just for the fun of it, over chips and sodas—and had made up things we had never actually experienced. The cold air was not as innocent as a child's lie, so one of us kept watch. We didn't want anybody to see us and start talking about us. We even tried to open the chip bags quietly.

Selim looked at the clouds while drinking his soda and afterward, having lowered his head, glanced at us with painful eyes. He probably thought his father was looking down at him. Perhaps his father was smiling at him the way Selim was smiling at us. He remained silent, a smile on his face, as we took turns. I chatted along too, but nothing I said mattered. What mattered was our common stance against pain. We were kids and wanted to remain kids on that cold pavement. There are times when everybody wants to be a child again, even people who experienced great pain in their childhood. You would have shared that feeling if you had sat on that pavement and had drunk soda with us. We all started laughing and punching each other when Veli, the quiet one, said, "You bastards! I saw how you ate the pastries this morning!" The chips dropped out of my mouth as I laughed.

Selim looked down and, with tears in his eyes, said, "Shh, be quiet."

We all paused. "Are you okay, Selim?"

He had been like a father or a big brother to us all that day. Above all, he was our conscience—the other half of our hearts.

"Be quiet. My father has just passed away."

Hello

I checked my mailbox as I left the house. It had been six months since I had last heard from my pen pal. Being pen friends with her had been a twenty-year addiction, twenty years of history. My pen pal had been a witness to the most important events in my personal history—to words and sentences that I could not even tell myself.

We had found each other during a school assignment twenty years before and had been using our sentences penned on white pages to compress the 500-kilometer distance between us. One day my literature teacher drew names in class and had assigned a pen pal for each one of us. It was an assignment that we all deemed as absurd, tiring, and unnecessary. In so far as I was concerned, sending letters was nothing more than writing Santa Claus wishes on the back of glittery cards.

We all reluctantly wrote a letter to an unknown person in the last half-hour of the class. What would you write to a person you don't know? "Hello, how are you?" Then you wait, think, and put down things about yourself. I wrote two pages all about myself; however, I realized how difficult it was to write to a stranger. Everybody in the class wrote something. Some wrote only half a page; some provided details about a soccer game between Beşiktaş and Fener.

It was important to write according to rules, to follow a certain page layout. The content was secondary. I was bored because I never liked those rules. Letter writing included everything one might hate about writing. We each put our letter in an envelope with an address on it and walked together to the post office to mail the letters. I wish we had had today's technology. It would have been great to take a selfie of us all licking stamps.

The responses to our letters reached our homes after a while. I have a clear picture of opening the letter while lying in my bed after dinner. It was a relaxed weekend. I'm not going to lie—I opened the letter with contempt; after all, it was from a little girl.

It started with "Hello." Contrary to my letter, which was all about myself, hers didn't say anything about herself. Yet I felt as if she were present in my room through her sentences. I'm not sure whether talent was involved, but would anybody good with words create a feeling like that? I pondered the letter and the sincerity of her writing for days. It was interesting to try to picture someone I didn't know. I wondered about her eyes, her voice, and her life overall, judging by her sentences.

I purchased a pack of white stationery and started writing without wasting any time: "Hello."

I wrote with excitement, and I put down hundreds of words for her without saying anything about myself. I felt so good sharing my thoughts and putting the images I'd seen into words. The secret chambers of my soul opened up; the new doors led to new hallways. I got to know myself as I wrote to her and established a close friendship with the new me. The more I wrote, the more I felt human and the more I felt like myself. Sometimes you share pain with someone, and sometimes you share the real meanings behind the sentences. Our sentences were defining us. With the lapse of time, we started completing each other's sentences. We agreed that we would not send each other pictures of ourselves. As technology progressed, we didn't search for each other on the Internet either. We had each other's name and address—and, most important, we had our writings.

We graduated from high school and started college. There were new people and new feelings in our lives. Trying to meet for tea in a café would have meant wasting all our sentences. Maybe we were both phony, playing the part of somebody else. I could have been playing the part of someone else, someone I would have liked to be. But our sentences were as similar as the lives of a couple married for fifty years. To have somebody akin to me 500 kilometers away made me feel that I wasn't alone. People are not lone beings; they shouldn't be. I realized that when I read her first letter twenty years earlier. I am grateful to my literature teacher because he provided me with more than what he had taught in class. I don't recall if the others wrote follow-up letters, but I was lucky at the time of that drawing.

I checked my mailbox as I left the house. Why hadn't she written? I used to keep track of the dates of her letters in my journal; she always wrote within two or three months. I had sent her three letters after her most recent one. She should have let me know if her address had changed. She had gotten married five years earlier and had divorced shortly thereafter. We continued to write to each other while she was married. I don't know whether her husband saw those letters or if he was jealous. She never said anything to that end. He would have seen two people trying to better themselves as human beings if he had seen them. Perhaps she had remarried. Perhaps her new husband was a jealous fellow. I chased the thoughts out of my mind because I didn't want to be the cause of any domestic violence.

I checked my mailbox as I left the house. I didn't want to go on having questions in my mind. I quickly devised a plan. My pen pal lived in Izmir. Yes, twenty years later, we were still 500 kilometers apart. I planned a short vacation. I had an address and a name, which I wasn't sure were real. I checked in at a hotel close to that address. To ease the excitement, I tried to convince myself that I was vacationing. I felt like a secret agent on the hunt for some secret organization. The straw hat and a pair of shorts were concealing the spy in me. I rehearsed what I would say when I saw her. My excitement was caught between my heart and my tongue. I began to feel regret. Perhaps I should go back; I shouldn't have come here. I should learn to live with what I had—the letters. Not knowing is good, provided it's not ignorance. It may mean pure happiness.

I couldn't know whether she had changed over the years or whether her face had wrinkled, for I had never met her. I had searched her name on the Internet, only to learn about her job—no photos, no detailed information. She could have disappeared as if she had never existed.

I went to the address on my second day in Izmir, with a smile meant to hide my excitement. I rang the doorbell and waited, then rang the bell again and waited some more. When nobody opened the door, I rang the neighbor's bell. An old lady opened the door and told me that the apartment was vacant—the people had moved; she didn't remember their names though. Then I rang other doorbells and asked other people. The more I asked, the more self-confident I became, asking ever more-detailed questions. Nobody knew where she had gone. She had lived there for two years, which I knew from the letters. I learned from the neighbors that she had lived on her own, was not married, and had no children. I felt relief and peace. I felt some kind of possessiveness due to the primitive codes in me that I couldn't even admit to myself.

I returned home a week later, after having failed to get answers from the market owner, the grocer, and the realtor. I started watching my mailbox again. Just as I was saying to myself that I should stop doing that, I found a note stuck between the door and the frame: "Hello . . . This is your pen pal. I came by every day for a week but wasn't able to find you. I know I haven't written in about six months. I've changed my address. If you are available this Sunday, let's meet at your favorite café. Hope you accept my apology. 2:00 p.m."

SILENCE

Was that a joke, or was my mind playing a game? I didn't leave the house that day, hoping she would return. I watched the street from the window. I even went outside and walked up and down the street. I wasn't able to sleep that night. I had a light Sunday breakfast and left for the café early. I was glad I hadn't had a longer vacation. I said to myself the metaphysician in me had made a correct calculation again.

I scanned the café as I entered. Maybe she'd come early too and was inside. There was nobody suspicious—no one other than the usual Sunday crowd.

"I'd like a cup of tea, please." The waiter didn't acknowledge my order but left a piece of paper on the table.

"A lady has asked me to give you this."

I looked around to see if she was watching me.

"Where is she now?"

"She stopped by early this morning, gave me this note, and left."

"How do you know it was for me?"

"You come here often. When she said your name, I remembered you."

The surprise on my face turned into the expression children have when on the verge of crying over a game they are losing. Note in my hand, I looked around again. I was certain she was watching me from somewhere.

"Hello, I thought it would be best if we didn't meet. Remember our promise. Let's continue with only our letters to each other. Here is my new address . . . Your pen pal."

A Brief Story about Love

I am painted in your colors,
I will not fade anymore
I am in love with you, I will not die anymore

—Yunus Emre, thirteenth-century
Turkish poet and Sufi mystic

Introduction

Do one's victories documented on paper make one a hero? Somebody turns up and settles in the best-guarded chambers of our heart with the speed of light. Our hero, even though he won't suppress our inner revolts, will hum the melodies of the most vivid songs at the borders of our inner space. Did Napoleon become Napoleon only because of his expeditions? A hero wouldn't be a hero—he wouldn't be able to touch hearts and souls—if he merely accomplished whatever he needed to accomplish to become a hero. He would be as superficial as an actor in a photo novel.

The heart emojis of social media condemn us to be dazzled with every *like*. We sway from side to side in our natural gas–heated homes as if dung were burning inside us. We search for love in our cellphones, and we design a new future for ourselves based on the sum total of *likes* we receive on social media. Hearts carved in trees with a Swiss Army knife are the reason Swiss scientists are unable to find the formula for love. Scientists are desperate . . . Minds that helped make the atomic bomb are desperate . . . Seasoned scientists are unable to discover something that will fuel our hearts. There is unfortunately no medicine we can place under the tongue twice a day to cure our laziness and lack of love. Is it that scientists are too lazy or that we are just used to living life in nine installments?

In a world in which everybody blames the next person, would the greatest poets of our time call upon our muse?

Development

High school years. The date is not important. However, if you really wish to find out, it was the period when one couldn't find any girl to one's liking in any social media account. It was the point in time when one had just entered adolescence, which guys do not wish to recall, the time frame when one looked at one's own pictures in disgust.

I was a sophomore in high school. My best friend was Mehmet. We were blood brothers even though we had not cut our fingers to allow blood exchange. We were in the same class. He was an introvert; I wasn't an outgoing person either, but somehow I ended up being the press secretary on every occasion. We were also neighbors. We helped each other in and out of class and during exams until the teachers started taking notice. We ended up making A's and surprised them. We laughed a lot; the least expensive thing to do was laugh. Despite those around us, who would tell us to be serious, we figured out new laws of laughter, thus proving that the laboratory was not the only place to study physics. When we committed errors, we didn't know what standard to measure them against. The concept of self-esteem would enter our lives years later. We converted our low self-esteem into national pride during the Street Fighter craze and said, "They have players from all over the world, but not us!" We chose Indian Dhalsim instead, to show support for those oppressed, like ourselves.

I'd always felt lucky to have Mehmet as a friend. I learned about sharing during those years. The future looked bright. We shared all our secrets. We would childishly tease each other about our weaknesses but would feel mature when talking about girls in plaid skirts. "Love" was a mere word, a form devoid of any meaning.

Conclusion

A new girl joined our class after the winter break. Her name was Bilge. I felt completely lost as soon as she slowly walked in my direction to take a seat diagonally across from me. Everything I knew got lost in her hair, in her walk, in her perfume spreading around the classroom and making her appear to be older than she really was. Within a quarter of a second, I admitted to myself that I was in love with her. To be platonically in love, to love from a distance, to be unable to sleep, to write love letters and not send them, to practice things to say and not utter them, all that was normal behavior for a high schooler.

I started laughing less now that I'd fallen in love. I would check whether she looked at me, and when she didn't, I would stare at her myself. Even a month after I first set eyes on her, I kept a distance, and when talking to her every now and then, I behaved as seriously as a man who'd saved the world. I wanted to surround myself with privacy walls lest she should see me. Consequently, I didn't tell Mehmet anything. All things morphed into their opposites; flavors and sounds got mixed up—desserts were salty, soups were sweet.

SILENCE

I spent a snowy weekend gazing through my window at a snowman outside, practicing what I was going to say to her on Monday. There are days in your life you never forget. That Monday was one of those days: the principal's usual start-of-week speech; permission for us to enter the classrooms in single file; math as our first class for the day; and Bilge, more beautiful than ever. I was going to talk to her between the math and literature classes. Years have passed, but everything in that lecture is still vivid in my mind. If anyone asked me to, I would be able to put down the Mathematics of Love in a flash. Which x would be most likely to intersect the unknown state of love in me?

Mehmet came over to me right after the bell rang. "Let me buy you a hot dog, Bro."

"I don't like hot dogs."

"A sausage sandwich then?"

I didn't want to have garlicky breath when I gave my romantic speech to Bilge.

"I'm not hungry."

"Come on, why are you so stubborn?"

I knew my friend. If he insisted, it meant there was something serious to it.

"I need to talk to you about something, Bro."

Despite my limited life experience, I knew that when someone said, "I need to talk to you," the listener couldn't expect to hear anything good.

"I haven't told you, but I'm in love," Mehmet said.

"Really?"

That one word was worth a page-long speech.

"Aren't you going to ask me with whom?"

"Bilge?"

"How did you know?"

Sometimes you don't want to know.

"Nothing escapes you, huh?"

"Yep. Nothing."

"I tried so hard to hide it from you."

"Hmmm..."

Sometimes there's not much else to say. In a world where there is no end to reality, I knew we were going to get lost in that well anyway, and I didn't want our few years of innocence to end too soon.

"Do you think you could talk to her on my behalf and see whether she's interested?" he asked.

The fact that he hadn't called me for a long time made me realize that he also must have been practicing his speech at home. I had kept quiet and had stayed away from Bilge for quite some time. My best friend, who became suspicious at my silence and at my lack of comment on his love, never raised the subject again. We did our best to find ways to get her existence out of our hearts as if we had signed a contract. Over time, flavors and colors slowly started sorting out. I began to taste the salt in savory food and the sugar in desserts.

One Monday—a Monday again!—we were in the gym. When the activities designed for us non-athletes ended, I partnered with Bilge during the stretching exercises. The soft spot in my heart also flexed as she was stretching my arms. I was unable to look into her eyes.

"Anything wrong? Don't we talk anymore?" she asked.

My arms were stretched and felt as light as cotton.

"Nooo!"

That also was worth a page-long speech. I was as red as my warm-up suit. When the class ended, I felt warmth in my ear.

"I love you, silly."

She ruined my soul by throwing her hair in my face, then entered the classroom without looking back. I experienced one of life's learning moments, right there in my red warm-up suit. I wish I could forget that Monday.

The following day I told her that I was in love with somebody else. After a long while, the high school rumor mill started spinning loudly. The sacrifice I had made for my best friend was the headline in the school's whisper newspaper. The freshmen declared me a hero, and I was respected. I was a rock star, not a high school student. I now entered the school like a marshal.

Years later, when Mehmet and I reminisced about that episode, he asked if I would do it again.

"I never meant to be a hero."

I recalled myself in the school corridors—a commander on horseback entering a city. Then I saw friendship in Mehmet's eyes and said with a blush on my cheeks, "I am a born hero!"

Bad Luck

The old man was not a regular at the table where I used to have tea. The "Ticket Man" used to go around selling tickets and reading poems but didn't normally stop by my table.[*] His hat with the National Lottery logo[†] on it didn't disguise the wrinkles in his face. The wrinkles gave away his age and the difficulties he had experienced in life. It was as if somebody had laid him down and made a carbon copy of his body

---

[*] Translators' note: Coffee houses and tea houses are very common in Türkiye. They are different from cafés, which sell food; only tea and coffee are served at tea houses and coffee houses. There are coffee houses in small villages and in every neighborhood of a larger city. Usually the same people go there every day, so everybody knows everybody.

[†] Translators' note: National Lottery tickets are sold in Turkish marketplaces, at street-corner kiosks, as well as by individual Lottery Office contractors. Such people walk around city streets and enter cafés, restaurants, and tea houses, selling tickets. New Year's Eve drawings are the largest ones of a year.

that he carried around, with the real body locked in a closet that smelled of mothballs at his home.

He first came to my table as I was taking a sip of my tea. He handed me some tickets with his aging hands.

"Here, son."

"No, thanks."

"The last three tickets."

"Thank you, I don't believe in games of chance."

His eyes glowed like a cat's. He held the tickets tightly and looked like a bill collector.

"Why?"

"I don't like them. I don't want to disturb my peace."

"The last three tickets. You should buy one."

"No, thank you, man."

Under his hat his head looked like it had been drawn using a sharp pencil. His face was pointy, his sentences were sharp, and his gaze was like a sponge. He would have laughed if I had laughed, and he would have sobbed if I had cried. The expression in his eyes was similar to the one displayed by people who had lived long and had experienced a lot. He handed me the last three tickets again.

"I don't want any."

SILENCE

"Why?"

"Ticket sellers usually save the last tickets for themselves. You should buy them, and if they are the winning numbers, let the winnings be all yours."

I had used hearsay information just to get rid of him. He put the tickets in his coat's inner pocket.

"I never buy the last tickets. In fact, I never buy tickets."

"How come?"

He moved the table he was leaning on with his hip and fell into the chair across from me like a dry limb. Suddenly his eyes turned into the eyes of a tiger that had just caught sight of its prey. Without saying a word, he ordered tea with a wave of his hand; the waiter nodded. He looked at me with a smile, but I could tell he was struggling to hold back tears. He sipped his tea with a serious look.

"Listen, son, I'm going to tell you a story. I usually don't tell this to just anybody."

His voice was peaceful. It had an instructive inflection.

"Year 1970. In those days, the jackpot stirred up everybody's excitement, and the rich and the poor alike awaited the day of the drawing. There lived a young man at that time by the name of

Fehmi, born in Aksaray, Niğde. When Fehmi turned ten, his father, fed up with relatives and neighbors, moved the whole family to Istanbul. Fehmi had a tough time and left school after eighth grade.

"Nowadays it's difficult to tell villagers from city folks, but in those days, they were different. Villagers were ashamed to go to a coffee house for a cup of tea. At any rate, Fehmi started selling lottery tickets in the daytime and driving a taxi at night. Keep that in mind.

"He was in love with a beautiful girl named Meral. In turn, the girl seemed interested in Fehmi, but she was a high school graduate, born and raised in Istanbul. There were a lot of young candidates who wanted her hand in marriage. Fehmi knew that her father would not approve of him. Fehmi and Meral would look at each other, showing interest, but they never spoke.

"Day by day, Fehmi became ever more in love, but he also liked the 'man in love' look in his eyes when he glanced in the mirror. His faith in life grew, and he started laughing more soundly when he laughed and crying more bitterly when he cried. In the worst-case scenario, he and Meral would run away, he thought.

"Her father was a retired police chief. His nickname was 'English Osman' because he was a very tall man with light-colored eyes and hair slicked

SILENCE

back with lemon juice. The neighbors knew he was coming because of the strong lemon smell. The business owners knew him from his days as a police chief and nicknamed him 'Stubborn Osman.' They rumored that his wife had died because of his stubbornness and she had whispered 'mule' into his ear when she breathed her last. It was also rumored that he had shown no interest in attending her funeral, but people had forced him to. That's why it was impossible to get him to approve Fehmi and Meral's courtship. Fehmi desperately waited for a chance to see and talk to her.

"One day Fehmi ran into Meral in a quiet place and had a chance to tell her that he loved her. She flipped her hair back and chuckled. 'You are wandering around our house a lot. If my father sees you, he will kill you.' Fehmi asked her to elope. She giggled and left with her hair and her body speaking a language he could not understand.

"Look, son, sorry if this story is taking too long, but when you tell a story like this in less detail, it tastes like sour apples.

"Anyhow, after many sleepless nights, Fehmi decided to talk to the girl's father. Consequently, he and his parents paid a visit to English Osman and, by God's will, made their intentions known. Osman kept his silence and dismissed them with his gaze. Deeply offended, Fehmi's mother later declared English Osman was 'a stubborn mule.'

"Well, Fehmi decided to elope with Meral, and it looked like she agreed. They would first go to Niğde, and then God knows where. Her father would be drunk on New Year's Eve, and they would leave while he was fast asleep. Once he went a-drinking, English Osman wouldn't know when to stop, and he wouldn't wake up even if Doomsday was to break out.

"Fehmi hadn't been able to sleep for days on end and had devoted himself to his work so as not to let anybody notice his excitement.

"On New Year's Eve, he went to the coffee house and waited amid the people drinking and dancing there. The big lottery drawing started on TV after midnight. The owner, Ibo, asked, 'Hey, Fehmi, how many tickets have you saved for yourself?' Fehmi had completely forgotten about the drawing; he was only thinking about Meral. Everybody was watching the TV screen, tickets in their hands. Just as he thought it was time and was getting ready to leave, Ibo asked again: 'Don't you have any tickets?' He didn't want to raise Ibo's suspicion by leaving that very moment. He knew Ibo would partner with the devil himself and might send word to Meral's father before they had even boarded the bus. As a result, he took his tickets out of his pocket and made his way closer to the TV. The numbers started showing up on the screen. He stared at his watch more than at the numbers.

"The speaker said, 'Seven, four, six, zero, five, five, six.' Fehmi cried out, 'God!' At first people didn't understand what was happening. He started screaming like crazy. He was about to lose his mind. Everybody started yelling, dancing, and celebrating. They carried him to his house on their shoulders in a very cheerful and festive spirit.

"While hugging his parents, Fehmi remembered Meral. He was rich now, so he went to her father and asked permission to marry Meral. English Osman gave him his consent. They had a big three-day, three-night wedding with lots of food and music.

"Fehmi loved Meral so much that no matter what she wanted, she got. She spent a lot of money helping distant relatives, helping young couples get married, or giving circumcision parties* for kids in the neighborhood.

"One day Fehmi received a notice that he was being called up for his mandatory military service. He had to go to Sivas and leave Meral

---

* Circumcision parties, following the ritual of a boy's circumcision (*sünnet*), are thrown by the family to celebrate the boy's first step to becoming a man.

behind. She wanted to start a business and asked for all his money. He was the kind of man who would do anything for the love of his life.

"After a hard, cold winter, just as Fehmi was counting down the remaining days of his service, Meral stopped answering his letters and phone calls. Worried sick, he asked his commander for permission to go to Istanbul, only to find his house vacant and no money in his bank account. Even English Osman didn't know where his daughter was.

"Fehmi considered not going back and becoming a fugitive enlistee, but his father made him go back. He reluctantly returned to his service and called his parents every day. He even telephoned Meral's father, hoping he would hear from her. They asked for the police and the gendarmerie's help.

"Fehmi learned the truth after he completed his military service and returned home. His father told him that Meral had taken all the money and left the country with another man. His mother called her a whore. Fehmi stayed silent; he did not say a thing. Soon he received the divorce papers. Those papers burned him the most.

"English Osman was so ashamed that he never left his house again. He got sick, lost a lot of weight, and died of grief. Nobody made his funeral arrangements; Fehmi had to see to the burial himself.

"Meral did not even look at Fehmi at the courthouse. She hired the best lawyer in the country and filed for irreconcilable differences. Fehmi was a proud person and agreed to whatever she wanted. People around him asked him not to give up his money, but he didn't care about money. He thought what happened to him had happened because of the money.

"He sold his house and started drinking and gambling. When he'd lost all his money, he returned to his parents' house. He started selling tickets again, for he did not have any occupation. The people in the neighborhood made fun of him for a while. He never bought the last tickets again. He always thought that if he hadn't won the jackpot, he would have been a happy family man now. He never said anything bad about Meral, even though he sometimes considered doing so. In short, he never felt low about losing the money—only about losing his love.

"I'm not sure if I explained things well, son, but that's why I do not buy the last tickets. Like you said, I don't want to disturb my peace."

The Ticket Man suddenly stood up from his chair like a spring stem.

"Okay, I will buy a ticket."

"You misunderstood me, son. I didn't tell the story to sell the tickets."

"Yes, I know. I want to buy a ticket."

"No tickets for you! Bye now. Thanks for the tea."

He left with the last three tickets in his hand. His story was haunting. My tea was cold. The waiter brought me a cup of fresh tea.

"Did he tell you?"

"What?"

"His story."

"You mean that was his own story?"

"Only a handful of people know it's his story."

"Really?"

"Just between you and me, Fehmi helped with my brother's circumcision expenses too."

While my surprise mingled with the sadness of a beautiful story, I could hear a voice outside.

"Last tickets!"

Misty Eyes

The bus managed to stop safely. Its old body was red, but its redness was not indicative of health. Its long body and its bellows caused people on it to dance to a different tune every time it braked or turned a corner. The buses had various names, and they would refer to each other by their names rather than by their assigned numbers.

The bus stopped safely, and the doors opened, giving out their habitual snoring hiss. I moved to the back of the bus along with the wave of people. My preference to sit at the back of the bus was an old habit dating back to my school days. It was due, in part, to the fact that it helped me show off my tall body, and, in part, to the perception that the cool guys always sat at the back of the classroom.

My watch showed a quarter before 8 a.m. It was perfect because two stops later, around 8 a.m., the girl with misty eyes would get on the bus. I had been watching her for two weeks. She was going to get on the bus and politely find herself a seat.

When the bus came to her stop and its doors opened without that loud hiss, the people in front of me prevented me from seeing her, but I knew she was on the bus because everything and everybody seemed to be moving in slow motion. The old bus was my good friend, and it proved its maturity. Who knows what it would say if it could talk?

I didn't know the girl's name. I just gazed at her. When I looked at her, it started drizzling even on sunny days. The clouds in her eyes would start a rain in my heart. Even though I didn't know her name, where she came from, or what her story was, I dreamed of scenes where she was the lead actress. Her misty eyes were present in my dreams. I would give her names and practice our first hellos.

"Hello."

"Hello."

There was no need for the rest. Any additional sentence would have diminished the expression in her eyes.

I was supposed to get off the bus three stops ahead of her, but I didn't, just to be on the same bus with her for a little longer. The stretches separating the three stops could cause a problem because the mist in her eyes could dissipate during the ride. I had already memorized the whole bus schedule. Our two-week-old story was as old as Adam and as unique as Eve. I had traveled to the most beautiful places in the world with her on that bus.

I was on the bellows' rotating part of the bus when, without even turning his head, the driver said, "Move toward the back." I made eye contact with her for a moment as the crowd started moving. One cannot see when eyes come too close.

I loved clouds. The clouds that rebel against the arrogance of the sun represented this girl's story. And her story was my story. We were actors in a most beautiful love scene. "Excuse me! What time is it?" she asked while looking at my watch. It was a quarter after 8 a.m., but the "quarter after" mattered not. She was going to get off at twenty after anyway. My inner recorder had already stored her voice. Her voice was going to be present in every sound thenceforth.

All I talked to my friends about was the girl. They were dying to meet her, because the lack of details about her was intriguing to them.

"What's her name?"

"I don't know."

"Did you talk to her?"

"No."

"Why?"

The answers to all those questions were in her eyes. I felt like I was watching the most beautiful scenery from the top of the world's most beautiful mountain. I wanted to grow something beautiful in the busiest parameters of the bus. Our first hellos should have lasted for a lifetime rather than merely for the short time needed to reach the last of the three remaining stops.

My friends, Hakan and Mehmet, started riding the bus with me, even though that was not their route. Curiosity was a good thing and so was loving someone from afar. Moreover, it was more exciting; the more I talked about her hair, her skin, and most important, her eyes, the more the girl in my story moved away from the bus and turned into a fairy-tale character whose name I knew not.

The vocal cords at the command center of my heart were cheering loudly. They appeared capable of translating "What time is it?" into Japanese. But it was only I who understood her language.

My story was in its third week now. This third week was the historic separator between the end of the Ice Age and the beginning of the next age.

Hakan and Mehmet were already waiting for me at the bus stop at half past 7 a.m. They had smirks on their faces. They looked like they were

SILENCE

there to steal something from me, and that something was not some collectible cards from gum wrappers. What I told them was my story. Actually, it was the story of the misty eyes; hence, it was her story.

The old red bus, whose name I didn't know, but which I recognized by the tear on its bellows, came at a quarter before 8 a.m. As usual, I made for the back. Mehmet and Hakan followed me closely. They were not familiar with the back of the bus because they weren't as tall as I was. They usually liked to stay close to the driver. They still had grins on their faces, displaying their thirty-two teeth.

It was almost a quarter after 8 a.m. The morning traffic was getting on people's nerves. My excitement created landslides inside me. When I saw Mehmet and Hassan's grins, the landslides eroded away.

When the bus halted at the stop where she was supposed to get on, we were all in a state of high alert. I was the head of the arrangement. The door hissed and made an awful noise as if it had lost all its bolts. As I was waiting excitedly, she got on hand in hand with somebody . . .

From that moment onward, the bus seemed to be even older, and it looked like the face of a mean old man on his deathbed. I could have hurt the guy who was holding her hand. I didn't like the expression on his face.

As Mehmet kept nudging me and asking "which one?" the bus seemed ever uglier; it became my enemy. The sun started shining even though the forecast had predicted rain. The clouds were dissipating.

Hakan must have caught my gaze and asked, "Is that her?"

"What?"

"Is she the girl with the misty eyes?"

There are moments where we don't need the truth. Dreams are at times more valuable than reality.

I turned to Hakan and said, "Today is sunny."

"What do you mean?"

"I mean, no, she is not! That girl is ugly."

The Child in Me

Heroes' tales, legends, stories, adapted over time, starting with Once Upon a Time, from 1001 Arabian Nights Folk Tales, Fables of LaFontaine, Stories of Dede Korkut, Tepe Göz, Keloglan to village theaters, or Red Riding Hood, Pinocchio, Cinderella, and Pollyanna, they are all our childhood heroes, guests in our invisible rooms. The cleaner our invisible guest rooms are, the more heroes we'll have to defeat the bad guys. Sometimes the heroes will be ourselves, and sometimes our fabulous friends. As we grow older, our heroes pack up and leave forever. We become arid, and our invisible rooms become empty. We should have special guest rooms like old ladies have in their houses, and we should leave the doors open, hoping that one day our heroes will come back.

It's Friday. I am in a taxi, sitting silently. The driver is minding his own business, smoking rather than looking at me. His unhappiness and anger are lingering on the seats, the mirrors, and the rosary by the gear stick. I open the window to inhale some oxygen, lest the high carbon monoxide ratio in the cab should cause any swelling in my diaphragm.

It looks like steam has been released from the driver's nostrils when the traffic suddenly stops.

"Ugh. Ugh!"

"It's like this on Fridays."

He lights up another cigarette passionately as if he were ready to trade everything in the cab for nicotine, then says, "You don't mind, do you?"

He takes such a deep breath from the cigarette that its redness reflects from the windshield onto our faces. The smoke goes into his lungs as if it were sorrow, anger, and bad experiences all at once and then comes back into the air like swear words.

"I wish we hadn't taken this route," he says while exhaling.

I don't take it personally, and I repeat, "It's like this on Fridays."

He doesn't answer, and I start reading old messages on my phone just to pass the time. Finally, the silence in the car is broken. First, the two-way radio beeps, then people are heard saying, "No, don't take that road." "Where are you?" The driver, unhappy with the noise, turns on the radio. He changes stations blindly, for all the dial markers on the old radio are gone. He finally finds a station and listens to commercials for about fifteen minutes as if he were listening to a lullaby. Meanwhile, we have moved forward by no more than 200 meters. The traffic then starts going, and he is happy to be able to shift to second gear. It is as if the blockage has cleared from our blood vessels and all our cells have started dancing. He enjoys his cigarette a lot more now, inhaling deeply so as not to offend his dancing cells.

I watch the taximeter as we approach the place I am headed for. It shows 28 Turkish liras. I take the money out of my pocket. I see a little boy's picture by the taximeter as I straighten the crumpled bills into their real values. I wonder how a sweet boy like this could be this mean guy's son. Then I think about the boy's mother and what my child will look like if I ever have a child.

"He is a sweet boy. God bless him."

"Who?"

"The boy in that picture."

"Ooh."

He smiles, showing me that he can smile.

"That's me when I was a little boy."

"Really?"

"Yes, it's me . . . I like this picture, and I look at it every time I am stressed and flustered. This is my only childhood picture."

"The only one?"

"Yep, only. . ."

We pass the place where I am supposed to get out. The taximeter now shows 32 Turkish liras.

"Only?"

"My mother burned all the pictures in the wood-burning stove by mistake. I had only four or five pictures anyway."

"So sorry. It's good that this one has survived."

"I've got five copies made of this one, just in case. . ."

"You did good."

What might have happened to this smiley-faced boy to cause him to turn into this grumpy guy? Maybe this photo captured his very last smile.

"Your smile is very nice."

He grabs his steering wheel tightly, as if holding on to his childhood, as he looks at his photo.

"This is what it is like on Fridays."

"Yes, it is like this on Fridays."

***

SILENCE

I call my mother as soon as I get out of the cab.

"Mom."

"Yes, son."

"Would you send me all of my childhood photos?"

"How come?"

"Particularly the smiley ones."

The German Shepherd

We lived on a construction site. When we looked out the window, we could see nothing but trucks and bulldozers. A subtle sound was touching the most sensitive part of our ears. The old houses were being torn down, and ugly buildings lacking even the meagerest trace of aesthetics were being erected. The grandchildren of Sinan* the Architect did not know how to build.

The building, at one time overpopulated with cats, got demolished. The roses that the old ladies had carefully kept had faded, and the beautiful garden was sacrificed to a parking garage. The 60-year-old building was torn down in two days. Big trucks blocked the street. The cats were nowhere to be seen. The building was old, and the paint had been peeling, yet I felt like that building had had a soul.

---

* Translators' note: Renowned 16th century Chief Ottoman Architect.

After the groundbreaking ceremony, a newcomer showed up among the bulldozers and excavators. It was a German shepherd, brought over to guard the construction site. He immediately informed the locals to heed him with the self-confidence of a German shepherd. He started barking at locals, passersby, cars, and, particularly, paper collectors.[*] One might have assumed that he had also memorized the license plates of cars. A major complaint started when paper collectors could not come near the street. Everybody knew that the paper collectors with their homemade carts cleaned the street. The complaints, shouts, and fights with the guard did not yield any results; the German shepherd was not to be taken off the street. When the officials from the municipality came, the dog disappeared and started showing up only after working hours. Between you and me, he also chased me at night several times. In spite of that, he didn't bark at children or families with kids; he stood in silence, bowing his head. I guess every living thing has a conscience. He was smart enough not to bark after certain hours in the evening. He knew he would be taken off the street. Nobody knew where he

---

[*] Translators' note: Poor people, mostly children, occasionally walk the streets of big cities with homemade carts and collect discarded paper and cardboard that they can make money on.

had come from or if he had guarded any other buildings before.

He had all the characteristics of a German shepherd. His hair, the brilliance of his colors, and the mischief in his eyes all indicated that he was a full breed. The other dogs and cats in the neighborhood had already left. The cats disappeared after the old ladies passed away.* The dogs fell victim to the German shepherd's invasion.

The new building's foundation was finished within a month. It was an ugly sight. The mix of concrete, steel rods, and wood looked like the skeleton of a human body. I wondered what material they were going to cover this ugly skeleton with.

Our German shepherd stopped showing up after dark. Knowing that he would chase me, I had started walking in a manner that brave men wouldn't be proud of whenever I had to pass the construction site. After a few days, I grew sure he had gone away, so I relaxed and my gait became manly again. Then one night he appeared from behind a car where he was hiding and started chasing me, barking loudly. I also heard him laughing. Yes, laughing! His voice reverberated in the street. Those at their windows and on their

---

* Translators' note: It is common in Türkiye to come across stray cats and dogs. People tend to take care of them just like the old ladies in this story.

balconies had lots of fun, but they did their best not to show their amusement, knowing it could be their turn the next day. Except for the strangers. When a newcomer walked down the street and our German shepherd started showing off, people openly laughed from their balconies. Our German shepherd would bark one last time and bow to the people for an encore.

As the building started rising, we started getting used to the dog. We had lots of love for him. He ensured the safety of our street. The ones who had complained the most were the first to give him food and water. He usually didn't eat right away; he would walk around for a while and show off. Then he would start eating slowly as if saying, "Since you insist. . ."

One morning we woke up only to discover that the whole neighborhood had gotten an awful gift. The building's exterior was complete. It had a mirrored facade that made it look like a business center. The expensive, sparkly material was unable to disguise its ugliness and callousness. This was how we were destroying the soul of the street and, most important, the city.

Our German shepherd had gotten so used to being on our street that he appeared sad to see the building completed. The mischief in his eyes was gone. He didn't bark at anybody anymore. He didn't bark at cars either. "Getting used to" must look like this. Once it makes it to your soul, it captures your whole body. I think every creature needs habits in their lives.

The construction workers and the guards had left, having returned to their hometowns maybe, but our German shepherd chose to become an expatriate. He disappeared during the night the guards packed up and left. He returned two weeks later with a special bark. We didn't know how he had survived. He was proud and walked away when asked about it. The whole neighborhood wanted him to stay. He also thought he had earned his retirement. He didn't want to be a guard dog on another construction site, get accustomed to a new street, and make himself accepted. He wanted to enjoy the peace that comes with familiarity.

The new owners started to move in. The cats showed up too, waiting for the old ladies to show up. They started chatting with our German shepherd while looking at the building without balconies. We learned later that the old ladies' children had sold their home, and the cats became the victims of the inheritance. The old ladies were not coming back. The cats were displeased to see the newly hung curtains, but they didn't leave the street. They were waiting for the old ladies more than for the food and the water. Setting aside the cats' discontent, our German shepherd had brought peace to the street.

You may be wondering whether this dog had a name. Although we had lost the old ladies and there were big, ugly condos in place of the old building, we had a German shepherd now. Yes, he did have a name. We called him Our German Shepherd.

Marbles

Three months after I learned to read, I received my report card, and summer break started. I left school with my buttons undone. My uniform was flying like a cape. It was a great visual for my perfect report card. My red "new reader" ribbon was not on my lapel anymore. I had my report card in one hand and my summer reading book in the other, and I was, of course, carrying my huge backpack as if it were a camel's hump. Even though it was the last day of school, my backpack was full of beans, colored paper, and such. There was no room for the summer book. My backpack was like a silo full of various beans.* But that had nothing to do with our brains turning into mashed beans as we grew older.

The book, which had been sold to us using high-level marketing techniques, was meant to be

---

* Translators' note: In the old days, kids learned math by counting beans.

our savior for the summer months. It was little more than a coloring book. It was to add fun to the hot summer days, but at the same time, it insulted our intelligence. The picture of a boy on the cover—you wouldn't want him as your child—was looking at me as if to say, "You're dumb." Okay, we hadn't deciphered the hieroglyphics, and we could only write very basic sentences, but we were humans after all. We would realize years later how much was expected of a generation entrusted to a summer reading book. I didn't like that book; it was a big disappointment as far as I was concerned.

I hid the book under my shirt while showing off my perfect report card at home. I couldn't toss the book because we had to return to school with it and prove that we had read it and had answered all the questions. I found a place in the glass-door cabinet in the living room to hide it, then I set all the whiskey bottles, now filled with tea, in front of it. I had drawn a mustache and a beard on the boy's picture. Two days before the end of summer break, I was going to answer all the questions. That was quite a plan.

The summer break was like free money: "easy come, easy go." Two weeks had already gone by before we started the marble season. The expatriates from Germany, who make the journey to visit family and friends every summer, had not arrived yet. It was fun to swallow (a humiliating way of saying "to win") their kids' marbles. My neighborhood was a hilly place, and playing marbles was very difficult. The kids from other neighborhoods were scared to be the visiting team. The big, contentious games could go on until dinnertime, until one of the mothers called. Those who play marbles know the game greatly depends on the ground. That's why pregame ground surveys are typically carried out by the older kids in the neighborhood. Our tiny hands could take on all geometric shapes. You needed to have firm thumbs for the "well game," strong wrists for the "pumpkin game," and good eyes for the "head game."

I wanted to make a quick start to the marble season. I started off with a small capital. We knew we had to yield to the conditions of the domestic market, that there would be no big market fluctuations before the kids from Germany arrived. I had one eye on the marbles, the other at Kapıkule border crossing.

I was checking on the summer reading book often. If my mother found it, not only would I kiss the marbles goodbye, but I would also be grounded until the kid on the cover grew up to be called to do his military service. At the same time, the mustache and the beard I had drawn on the boy would reduce to zero how responsible I was in my mother's eyes.

My hands started cracking and flaking off with the heat of the summer as the home and away games went on. During the "well game" in particular, we would dig our hands into the ground, and they'd take up the color of the soil. I used to soak my hands in Murphy's Oil soap so my father wouldn't take note during dinner. The tanned face and neck, the rough, cracked hands that resembled chicken feet represented the epitome of my summer. My small capital had started to grow; the marbles hidden in the shoe cabinet were now expanding into the winter shoes. I was proud of my success. I would have liked the boy on the cover of the book to witness it.

It was becoming difficult to hide the marbles in the evening. God forbid, if my father had seen them before the kids from Germany arrived, I would have been banned from the games by the Local Court.

We were halfway through the summer break. My hair was long enough to be combed into styles now. My image in the mirror looked a little grown. My, it had been four months since I had learned to read! My mother made me read the newspaper during breakfast. That was my only education. I was not into books. The protagonists were either at the beach or somewhere else, vacationing pleasantly. It was easy for them to take part in conversations under a beach umbrella while my vacation was being spent on sandy ground, playing marbles. Life would soon enough teach me to take interest in things I hadn't experienced.

There was a stir in the neighborhood when the families from Germany arrived. The German cars looked down on our domestic cars. I wouldn't have wanted to witness a car get so humiliated. The German cars with their brawny muscles took up as much space as their owners' bellies. We would have taken selfies in front of the German cars, had mobile phones been invented. But neither technology nor German cameras made that possible. One of the expatriates with a beer belly made us line up in front of his car and took a picture. We lined up like penguins and smiled like humans.

"I will send you all a photo," he said.

But he never did. That photo showing me with marbles in my pocket vanished into thin air. It is unfortunate, for we all smiled nicely for it. We were hoping that the expatriates would return permanently. Who would leave this beautiful country?

Toward the end of summer, I had bags full of marbles. I sold some of them at a discounted price. I understood how the banking system had been created. It was difficult to hide so many marbles. I had to watch my back and hide them in secluded places every evening before dinner.

My mother happened upon the book about a week before the end of summer break. She also found the marbles. I think the boy on the book cover told her. My father made the official announcement of my collapse and my bankruptcy.

"School starts next week. Take these marbles to wherever you wish and do not bring them back. Look at your hands; are you a beggar or a schoolboy?"

The marbles in the house were one-tenth of what I had. I still had an entire treasure under trees and in the attic. The kids from Germany had lost all their marbles.

There was one more week before school started. My long, wavy hair was now trimmed very short. I wasn't in a good mood. I was to go home before dark and answer the questions in the summer reading book. My spiritual and physical bonds with the marbles had been severed. My parents were right. I needed to get ready for school; what would I need the marbles for?

I put together an announcement for the kids in the neighborhood. I would be climbing the highest hill and giving out all my marbles without any intent to cheat.

I was there at the promised time. There came a gigantic crowd. Kids had come from other neighborhoods even. The kids from Germany

SILENCE

were there too, hoping to get some of their marbles back. In their eyes, I was a mad man who was giving out his wealth.

I had the marbles in two big black bags so the kids couldn't see them. The older kids had warned me that if the whole thing proved to be a hoax, they would fling me down the hill like a marble. I knew they would; one couldn't joke about marbles! I stood on my toes on a rock and flung away handfuls of marbles. Everybody was scrambling, pushing each other, and trying to grab the marbles. I flung them ever farther away, for the crowd had become scary. I could have flown like a bird, or my elbows could have shot into the clouds like arrows. I was scared, sad, and elated at the same time. Ridding myself of those marbles, which I had won fair and square, was creating egocentric stirrings in my little self. I was throwing the marbles so far that kids had to run across two neighborhoods to grab a marble.

When I made it home, my father had a hammer in his hand and nails in his mouth. The way he had placed the nails at the edge of his mouth showed that he was angry.

"What's happened, Dad?"

"We have a broken window. Some vicious fella hurled a marble from that hill."

Hasan, Son of Ahmet

Despite his dark, thin, skinny face, the energy in his eyes was enough to illuminate an entire city. He was the nine-year-old son of a family who had migrated from the very east of Turkey to the very west.

He was unlike the other kids who stopped you in the street to sell you facial tissues. He stood before me like a career boy ready for a job interview. Our first meeting was a little formal, but afterward, whenever I stopped for a cup of tea, he would come to my table. He didn't answer questions with questions; he used his own answers as questions. You got no hint of family troubles either in his voice or in his gaze. He didn't speak much; when he did, he created a velvety softness between an individual's face and their conscience. His short life of nine years—six years in Kars and the latest three in Istanbul—had exposed Hasan to experiences more common among people aged in the double digits.

He would quietly approach my table whenever he saw me. He would walk on tiptoe when there were other people at my table. There is no age to be graceful. Dignity is neither in someone's voice nor in their looks. Dignity can surface when you least expect it: in a nine-year-old boy, the son of Ahmet.

"Hasan, what do you want to become in the future?"

He laid the packs of tissues on the table and answered as if he had never been asked that question before.

"I don't know exactly what, but it is going to be a good thing."

"A good thing . . . What does 'a good thing' mean?"

"I don't know, something good."

He did not say "a doctor" or "a pilot." I understood—or at least, so I thought—that what he was unable to put into words was that he simply wanted to become a good human being. He could be a doctor or a pilot as long as he was a good human being.

"You hang around here quite late, until dark. How do you get back home?"

The answer to this question made me notice the many other kids like him around.

"We live in Umraniye, and there are no buses at night. So we, the group of kids, get together every night and take a taxi. We pay ten liras each. The taxi driver is our neighbor, so he gives us a discount."

"That's cool."

"Well, it's not if I don't sell enough packs of tissues."

Talking about people's pains and listening to people referring to their pains may be valuable at times. But Hasan's story—his father's joblessness, his mother's illness, their migration from Kars—was to be perceived as a profoundly intimate story.

"How do you like Istanbul?"

No matter how much he may have liked Istanbul, when he talked about Kars and the village he was born in, there was a dusty village road running deep within him. It surfaced when someone grew angry with him and insulted him; he used to run down that dusty road, connecting his heart to his mind.

Hasan, son of Ahmet, became a good friend of mine. Sometimes I went out for tea merely to talk to him. We would have our daily talks and share the sin of childish gossip. When he was mad at someone, he didn't curse the way the other kids did. He kept to himself such cuss words, uniting his heart and his tongue as if feeling ashamed.

Once the feeling of shame enters a person's soul, it travels like a worm inside an apple, reaching the core and becoming an integral part of the person. Shame is a positive feeling to have, and it was the feeling to best describe Hasan. Good things suited Hasan best, despite the instances where his cheeks went red and he became unable to challenge anybody.

Our friendship lasted for one-and-a-half years. I last saw him in September; it was raining, and we greeted each other and shook hands like grown-ups. I never saw him again after that rainy day. I asked everybody about him, from the Flower Boy to the Bagel Boy. I wondered if something had happened to him. I hadn't heard anything about his brother either.

The only thing I knew about them was that they lived in Umraniye, for Hasan didn't like to talk about himself. In the huge city of Istanbul, Umraniye could easily become larger than Istanbul. I checked all the taxi companies in Umraniye and asked about a driver who would give kids a free ride every night. I finally found him and listened to the story of Hasan, son of Ahmet, as told by him. The taxi driver was not comfortable at first, but once he realized I was determined to know things, he agreed to answer my questions.

"I usually pick them up as my last job of the day, for I live in the same neighborhood."

SILENCE

"Where is Hasan? Have you seen him?"

"Is he the skinny one with an older brother?"

"Yes, he does have a brother."

"They went back to their village."

"To Kars?"

"I don't have the details."

Hasan, son of Ahmet, went back to his village. Was his story supposed to end here, or did he go back to his village to write a new story? I would miss him as well as our conversations.

I was heartbroken, yet I knew he would find his way along that dusty village road. I had just completed a story about someone named Hasan when I heard the terrible news on TV: Somewhere in the countryside, several children had died in a dormitory fire. Those words lost their meanings. What I saw and heard created waterfalls that cried within me. I turned off the TV and started a new story, another story about Hasan.

For the best stories are the rewritten ones.

With a Smile

The telephone kept ringing and ringing. My hands were tingling. Nails were holding my neck and body together as if I were made of wood, like Pinocchio. My fingers kept splintering against the phone's Answer key; my fingertips were smacking my knotty neck, turning my body into a carpentry shop. I knew what was about to happen. I started liking Pinocchio even more as I cursed his creator for not having solved the "nose" issue. I didn't mean the fairy-tale side of the lie, but the real-life equivalent of it. After twelve missed calls, I answered the phone, stopping the ring-ring that had converted my body into a carpentry shop.

My past, present, and future friend Hakan was the caller. I listened to him in prolonged silences. I knew exactly what he was going to say. One can recognize old friendships by the moments of silence during conversations. I knew what was going to happen and silently practiced my lies. My brain was a stage, and my frontal lobe was a bad actor. I couldn't do that.

Hakan loved Aslı. I was friends with Aslı and good friends with Hakan. Hakan wanted to take action that night and play the season finale of an ineffable confession of love. I had no need to hear the end of the story. Aslı was leaving. She was going to study abroad. Hakan was saying, "She is leaving, buddy. I will tell her everything at dinner tonight." And, for fear of losing his love, he kept praising his country's schools.

I embraced silence as my savior and said nothing. I just produced an occasional "hmm" and waited for his anger to cool. To Hakan, "hmm" was the most fabulous word in the world. As my phone battery was about to die, I still tried to produce my "hmm," articulating only one "m" though. I envisaged myself as a sheep at the sacrificial market.

I contemplated the time and the place of the dinner and even our seats at the table. I arranged everything as a result of a great deal of green-colored message exchanges and "read" designations on my phone. Our round table, involving a friend, a lover, and me, was ready for everything. I didn't talk much. Hakan was also silent, but he was talking with his heart in a pose suitable for people suffering from love.

SILENCE

Aslı talked about the city she was going to, providing all the details just like a tour guide and pointing out the time zone difference between the two cities—the main topic of conversation at the table. The clock was ticking, and the deeper the conversation grew, the quieter Hakan became. Between references to museums and exhibitions, Aslı mentioned in passing someone in her life. All of a sudden, she was elevated from tour guide to woman. I suppose Hakan heard the last sentence in Chinese, for he cut a big piece of fatty meat and stuffed it in his mouth.

I just kept saying "hmm." I enjoyed producing those "hmms. " I looked at him discreetly. I felt like reading the pages of a script over and over again. Everyone and everything kept silent; the sounds of the forks and knives were turning into the sounds of Hakan's heartbeats. I also stuffed meat in my mouth with the weariness of what I knew and what I was yet to see. I was not sure if the "hmms" had to do with the meat or the situation we were in. "Hmm" became the summary of the night.

Aslı told us about the man she loved, how nice he was to her, and how he was also going to move abroad with her. She pounded all this into Hakan's head. We engraved the guy's face in our memory. We could have gone and killed that man with the bitter turnip taste* that prevailed in our mouths.

Hakan had a strange look on his face as a result of his heart's indigestion. His expression resembled the gaze of poor peasants who had seen Khidr.†

When the check came, Hakan slapped our hands and quickly paid for the dinner with the frenzy of a person suffering from heartache. He considered that the suffering of all humankind had turned into his own pain and showed no empathy toward the waiter. The word "silence" was alive and well at that moment, breathing quietly at our table. As we drank our tea, Hakan had a brewed smile on his face that transferred its meaning and its importance to the tea. He kept looking at Aslı, perceiving the noises made while stirring sugar into his tea as his heartbeats.

I didn't need to learn the end of the story. When I looked at Hakan's face, I saw the most naïve face a man can have. With a smile.

---

* Translators' note: Turnip juice (Şalgam Suyu) is a popular beverage in southern Türkiye; people who drink it are occasionally associated with machoism and the readiness to fight and kill.

† Translators' note: Servant of God, made reference to in the Quran.

The Old Woman

The rifle was invented, bravery was lost;
Now the sword should rust in its scabbard . . .
—Köroğlu, sixteenth-century semi-mystical
hero and bard

The rifle was invented; bravery was lost. Google was invented; the encyclopedia was lost. They are yellowing in cardboard boxes now. The once-attractive source of information has departed from our living rooms. The information entered in our phones has started smelling like garbage in our palms. Therefore, now the sword should rust in its scabbard.

A car drove by us, raising a cloud of dust behind it. "Look at that car. It's a diesel," said Hakan with his ever-present smile on his face, overinflating the car's worth. It was good to have something to talk about on the way to school. The road was dusty, but our feet were ready to slip and swing like in a dance. Talking about cars while walking was like paving the dusty road. There were empty lots between buildings, and empty lots equated playing soccer. Hakan and I looked at each other. Ours were the looks of two kids who really were meant to be kicking the ball.

Hakan threw his bag in a corner and ran onto the field, urging me to kick the ball toward the goal. He said, "*Metin, Ali, Feyyaz,*" which meant, "Goal. . ." I ran behind him. I took off my necktie, tied it like a squad captain's band onto my arm, and passed him the ball. Our sweaty armpits and necks filled the air with an adolescent smell. The geography teacher could teach the map just by looking at our faces. Hakan's face looked like an African desert; mine resembled the reddest parts on the map. We didn't know who we were playing against, but everybody was excited to be kicking the plastic orb. It was more of a javelin-throwing event than a soccer game.

We were happy, and there was physical comfort in not attending the first class. That comfort had nothing to do with the fact that the first class was physics. It was just the joy of cutting class and playing in the dusty field. Another fact was that passing the ball to the kids from your own neighborhood had become an official obligation, and the footprints on your school pants were stamps of other neighborhoods.

SILENCE

After running and sweating a lot, I leaned against a wall. I licked the beads of sweat from my face and nose. I was so thirsty that I didn't notice the old woman next to me. In fact, I was so thirsty that the whole world seemed to have vanished.

"Hi, son."

When I looked up, I saw two beseeching eyes staring at me and an old body.

"Yes, ma'am."

"Don't mistake me for a beggar."

The mere fact that she used that word was an indication that she wanted something. Her husband had passed away the previous year, she had had to pay for her good-for-nothing son's bills using her retirement fund, and she had come to see herself forced to ask for help from everybody, even from me, the sweaty kid. I felt very sad. She was asking for money for her medicine. I was a student, so my allowance wouldn't have been enough for a placebo, let alone for medicine.

I hollered for Hakan. He looked up and understood the situation, so he came over at once. The old lady told him her story too. Our eyes were watery now, as if our sweaty faces were not enough. Hakan and I looked at each other. We had to help her to at least buy medicine. As the sweat on my skin cooled off, I forgot that I had been thirsty.

Hakan and I were playing a game with our eyes in which no one had scored yet. Then he whispered in my ear, "You get your piggy bank, and I will fetch my brother's hidden money." What he said created a Robin Hood effect, and I responded, "Okay."

There was a problem though. Our first class was physics, my mother was at home, and the piggy bank was in the living room—the centermost room of the house. Hakan's face had an unexpected serious look, as if he had solved the problem.

"We will say we've forgotten our homework assignments."

Why hadn't I thought of such a simple plan? The jealousy of not being able to solve simple matters sojourned in my body for some two to three seconds.

"Just wait here. We'll be right back," I said to the old woman. She had an I-can-wait-forever expression on her face as she sat on a rock.

Fueled by that look, we ran to our homes. I grabbed the piggy bank, and Hakan stole his brother's money. Were we going to steal our offspring's money and become worthless individuals in the future?

On our way back, Hassan had another idea. Our neighbor, Nesrin, was a nurse at the health center across the road. We could take the old lady to the center and have her examined. It was Hakan's day for good ideas, but I too proved kind enough to take the small change out of the piggy bank, exchange it for bills, and put the money into an envelope. We took the old lady, who was waiting for us on that rock, to the health center. She agreed to whatever we said, becoming the youngest voice of our conscience.

While Hakan was inside talking to Nesrin, I gave the old woman the envelope with the money. Her eyes were in tears, so I felt like I would break the piggy bank again.

Hakan leaned out of one of the windows of the center and asked me to come in. Inside, the health center looked like an old photo from World War II of crying babies, sick children, and sick people in general, all waiting in line. Nurse Nesrin told us about the waiting time, but also asked us why we were not at school.

When we went back to where we had left the old woman, we were unable to find her. We looked for her in the bathrooms, in the courtyard, in the hallways of the health center, and even on the soccer field. We reached the following conclusion: The old woman didn't want to be ashamed and offended any more. We had been bad kids. We had embarrassed her. We had been inconsiderate. Piggy bank breakers today, bank robbers tomorrow.

The next day we related everything to everyone in our classroom. They were all interested in the old woman's story. We had kids waiting in line to help her, were we to find her, eager to steal their dad's money if it came to that. Some of our teachers also expressed their wish to contribute.

Every day thereafter, we stopped by the dusty field on our way to school. The rock the old woman had sat on became like a shrine. In truth, we had also organized a mystical trip for our friends there. We had been singled out as kind, generous thieves in the school hallways.

***

Every story needs a dénouement. We came across the old woman months later in a different place. We cried out in joy that we'd found her. We had questions for her. Had she gotten her medicine? What had happened to her good-for-nothing son and her retirement money?

"Where have you been, ma'am?"

She looked at us with surprise and said nothing. Hakan understood everything, and his smile turned into a straight line. I saw the opposite of what she had conveyed to us through her silence. We had looked for her for days and had hoped that her story was true. Whom could we trust, for whom could we steal a piggy bank henceforth? I still think those piggy banks should be stolen and be used for charity when time is ripe. I asked her if she had gotten her medicine. The surprise on her face has stayed with me to this day.

We were unable to be angry with her and refused to play any part in her shame. Our deceived young selves did not want to face the truth. We wanted to create a new truth by believing our own lie. I don't even wish to talk about her face when we told her about the school principal's help. Everybody, from the principal to the neighborhood business owners, had heard her story. Some guys had even put together a plan to beat up her son. The story grew in the telling; now people were talking about a drunk son who would beat up his mother. We concocted a dramatic story to conceal the stupidity with which we had exaggerated her problems once we realized we had been deceived. We didn't want to be known as victims who had stolen money from a brother and had broken a piggy bank. Creativity and gossip had no limits in such situations.

The old woman never said a thing to us. We answered our questions ourselves, assuming she was too ashamed to answer. We were like candidates in city board elections making empty promises. We were even going to buy her furniture—despite not having credit cards!

The old woman straightened the scarf covering her hair and uttered a single sentence.

"Where do you live?"

Hakan stretched out his arms. "Up there, at the end of that street. Our houses are across from each other."

The old woman's eyes were glowing. She wanted to meet the parents who had raised such kind, generous kids. Since we were like that, what would our fathers not do, what would our mothers not give?

We kept the hurt inside. Our cheeks displayed the color of shame. I guess there surfaced a primitive pleasure of being deceived. And trying to be a good person was raising the threshold of pleasure.

The old woman turned around and started climbing the hill.

"Don't forget! The first house on that street."

The Smell

Years ago...
There was a smell coming out of my school bag. Figuring out the source of the smell took the amount of time a bright student needs to memorize the times table.

The smell coming forth from my notebook spread all over my bag, making it appear to have bidden me farewell and have come to belong to somebody else. The smell was coming from the scented eraser that used to belong to Ayca, who sat next to me in the classroom and whose front teeth had been eaten by a mouse. The smell from the pages of the notebook was creating a scented world for the boy studying at his desk at home. The relationship between erasing and that smell was more a matter of life science than of philosophy. In a way, "to erase" meant "to hide."

I collected memories starting with the smell coming from that notebook the way others collect stamps. It was the beginning of a passion that was to become the most beautiful pastime in the world. Oh, how much I recorded while erasing a wrongly placed comma! Ayca's eraser turned into the world's most powerful recorder. That must be why all the things I ever tried to erase from my life had a smell. Trying to erase things was a superhuman action, and life did not accept grammar mistakes such as a wrong comma. I probably wouldn't remember Ayca's face, but everything I had shared during the school years was, later in life, connected in my mind with that smell.

Years later . . .

I was in the "worst-sellers" section of a bookstore and was very distracted. It felt like a grocery store rather than a bookstore. I was undertaking a literary journey along the aisles. When I returned to the Turkish literature section, my clothes and hands smelled like perfume. I sniffed around to figure out whether the scent was coming from the girl by the self-help books. The fragrance got stronger as I walked around, as if my own breath was spreading "perfume monoxide." Why did this smell surround my whole body with heart-shaped, scented boundaries?

I left the bookstore and entered the restroom of the cafe across the street. I meant to rid myself of the smell by washing my hands and face. When I made eye contact with myself in the mirror, I splashed a handful of water on my face in hopes that it had all been a dream. I was brought back to reality by a knock on the door. I freed the bathroom for the guy at the door without drying my face, which still smelled of perfume. He couldn't not have smelled the perfume, and sharing her scent with the man brought the word "jealousy" back into my life. I walked quickly and continued sniffing the air around me. I wanted to go home and take a shower to get rid of the smell. When the records of memories were opened, the world potentially became a perfume-filled cauldron.

As my nose was becoming ever more tired, I caught sight of one of those friends you usually run into at the most ridiculous moments.

"What's up, man?"

Using one of those cliché answers, I said, "Nothing much. You?"

"I'm fine. Let's have some tea if you're not busy."

"I have to go home."

"Just one cup."

"Say, do I smell?"

"Like sweat?"

"Don't you smell it?"

"Nooo. . ."

The nooo involving three o's confused me. His nose must have been blocked.

"You mean there's no smell coming from me?"

"Nooo..."

I left him and returned to the bookstore. I knew what I needed to do. I needed three things, but I was specifically looking for a scented eraser. The erasers in different colors and in the shapes of cartoon characters whose names I didn't know smelled like detergents. I found an eraser that smelled like Ayca's. I also bought a notebook and a pencil before leaving the bookstore.

At the table, pencil in hand and a white page in front of me... The scented eraser was the guest of honor at the table, aware of the importance of how it would be used, like actors of all lead roles. The scent had become a part of me and had begun painting the table. I started writing about the source of the smell. How we met, the first sentences, the hello...

HELLO

HELLO

I wrote a few pages before having half of my cup of tea. The harmony created by beautiful sentences was coming out of the dungeons in my mind. I didn't want to erase anything; everything was real as depicted. While writing about her scent, I was describing all the flowers without ever making use of a comma.

HELLO

Everything carried on with the innocence of a hello. I didn't have a vocabulary to write bad sentences. As I wrote, I felt the scent surrounding my body dissipate. The scent of basil permeated all the predications. The nobility and fierceness of the predicates surrendered to the authority of the subjects.

HELLO

I was underlining it as the most beautiful love-expressing word in the world. I was aware that certain words had their scents and that the rooms of poets smelled so good that no perfume brand could emulate it.

I did not drink the tea in front of me, for specific sentences were to be used when one drank tea. One could be more infused than the present time. The sound made in the cup by the teaspoon was more effective than the modern notifications for time and place. I had a wide grin on my face, a grin spread from ear to ear.

When I looked up, I made eye contact with the same friend I had seen earlier. My grin slipped through my teeth to my internal organs. He came over and spoke to me, using elusive intonations.

"What happened? I thought you were going home."

"I decided to have a cup of tea."

He quickly pulled up a chair.

"I would like to have one too."

Then he suddenly got up and started breathing like a bull.

"What's this, bro? Have you bathed in perfume? You smell!"

I regained my grin.

"Nooo..."

The Snowman

If he laughs well, he's a good man.

—Fyodor Dostoyevsky

I never ask myself how to identify good people . . . Is good people's way of laughing less effective than bad people's mouthfuls of drool and noise effects? Even though every question might get a response, no questions are to be asked after a good laugh.

He stopped by and poured out his heart right onto the table. He had a mischievous look in his eyes like the one elderly ladies have. He was eight years old, too young compared to me.

"What's up?" I asked with the pride of the one having turned nine not long ago.

He talked about his New Year's Eve plan slowly, chewing his words as if he had breadcrumbs in his mouth. We were going to set a "Welcome, 1990" on the window. We were going to bury the '80s in the darkness of history using the cotton and glue he had stolen from his mother's drawer.

Hakan had mapped it all out. Our families would gather in my family's apartment, and the living room window would be presented at night. Lots of tabouli, some tangerines, bingo, and then straight to bed. We wouldn't forget to make it look like it was snowing, using the carefully balled-up cotton. We decided to make it artificially, even though the snow outside was a cruel reality. We still had years to wait for the Japanese glue* to come into our lives, so Japan still meant Barış Manço† for us.

Hakan couldn't sit still. He wanted to do a great many things, as if having overlooked that he was only eight years old and was waiting for someone to remind him. The snow outside not only poked fun at the flecks of cotton we'd stuck to the window, but also spoke of the '80s. We would, maybe, miss the modest, humble '80s, but we had high expectations of the '90s. We could never have foreseen how the 2000s would belittle them.

---

* Translators' note: Superglue is popular in Türkiye.

† Translators' note: Well-known Turkish singer-songwriter who went on tour in Japan in the 1990s.

SILENCE

Hakan explained his second plan as we were wiping the glue off our hands. "And we'll make a snowman!" At midnight, we would take everybody to the back yard and show them our snowman. It was a cool plan, and it would add a high-resolution visual to the unpretentious, single-channel TV life of the '80s.

Special days added color to our peaceful solitude and enabled us to collect carloads of memories. I stole a carrot from the fridge—the same way Hakan had stolen cotton from his mom. I also stopped by the coal shed and carefully hand-picked some coal on account of aesthetic concerns.

We shoveled the snow in the back yard and used it to make a large trunk for our snowman. Hakan was on his knees acting out his "I'm tired!" thing, demonstrating yet again how laid-back of a kid he was. I made the second ball of the body and used my near-frozen hands to finish the finest areas between the neck and the abdomen. It was getting dark. I picked up the pace, because my hands were getting ever colder, and with surgical precision molded the snowman's face, making it more human in appearance: perfectly smooth white skin, two eyes made from small pieces of coal, and a smile made with smaller pieces. My snowman smiled so nicely that the blackness of the coal pieces warmed me up. I refined my glowing snowman, using the carrot for a nose and adding a broom as part of his body.

My snowman was the only thing I ever had liked before turning nine. My crayon drawings and the potato prints I used to make at school looked like odd pieces from the Stone Age compared to my snowman. The human instinct to create something and the admiration for the creation may start expressing itself with a carrot and smiling fragments of coal from Zonguldak.[*]

The sound of the countdown for a new year caused a lot of excitement in our single-channel TV life, one that used to calm us down and put us to sleep. The whole city of Ankara, with its boulevards and streets, glowed like it was eight years old, having waited for this day its entire life. Obviously, we did not like the '80s.

As the winning lottery numbers were announced on TV by a speaker who was showing off all the subtleties of the Turkish language, there followed a not-winning silence through the house.

Our mothers' food, the smell of the oranges, and we, the children, who had switched from playing Parcheesi to bingo so we wouldn't fall asleep, we were all avenging ourselves on the '80s. 10, 9, 8, 7, 6 . . . The start of a new year, the

---

[*] Translators' note: Mining region in Türkiye.

hope-filled hugs we gave each other, and our irrational faith in the future showed us that we were apt to remain human, despite everything.

Before making it to the most inviting hours of sleep, we took everybody to the back yard. Our siblings, parents, grandmothers, and aunts all came out. We also had spectators on balconies who had had too much to drink or were sneaking a puff of cigarette. The back yard turned into a fairground.

Hakan's father asked, "So?"

I pointed to our surprise and said, "There. "

All the heads in the neighborhood turned as I turned to look at my snowman. After a brief silence, I walked over to my snowman only to notice that the carrot had turned into a sexual organ and his smiley face had turned into the face of a disgruntled kid. Those resentful kids from the other neighborhood had humiliated my snowman in front of everyone, down to the drunk Uncle Semih in one of the balconies. The loud laughter of the crowd and the grumbles of old ladies showed that one could still be ashamed of a carrot.

I had tears in my eyes, yet tried hard not to burst out crying. I didn't like the '90s. I wanted to forget this night by going to bed right away and pulling the covers over my head. I was more upset about what had happened to my snowman than by people's laughter.

My snowman had had such a beautiful smile; I wish everyone could have had a smile like that. It was as if something had been whispered in my ear, to my young soul.

I had made that smile from the smiles I had collected for years. I continued collecting smiles from the faces I loved for as long as I breathed. At times, they were embedded next to a dimple on my lover's face; on other occasions, with the hand extended by a friend; but most important, they were my own smiles when I watched myself in the mirror.

I was going to make a better smile for my snowman the moment I woke up. I awoke to my mother's voice. It was past noon. I looked at the clock and yelled, "My snowman!" As I was bolting out the door, I saw the water droplets on the window. My whole body froze. It had rained, and the snow had melted. The tears that had been waiting inside me since last night streamed down my face.

I ran to the back yard and found the bits of coal, the carrot, and the broom observing a moment of silence for my snowman on the wet ground. I heard my mom's voice and felt her presence behind me as I picked up the coal. "Come inside, you'll catch a cold."

SILENCE

Looking at the pieces of coal in my hand, as if talking to my snowman . . .

"Mom, do good people always have nice smiles?"

"Where did that come from? Who told you that?"

"My snowman, who else?"

To Leave

She used to hide behind sentences. I, on the other hand, used to raise icebergs of unspoken words.

She spoke for a long time without taking a breather between sentences. "Well, I'm leaving," she said.

Does the verb "to leave" always have to be so cruel? Time and place had no importance. We were sitting at a table and set our primitiveness on fire with the help of the babbling of modern-age noble people. Once the verb "to leave" had been uttered, all the forthcoming words rolled downhill like a runaway truck. We expressed our past griefs and sorrows chronologically, equating them with humanity's sufferings throughout history. When saying "we," I meant "she." I only listened and became a partner in shame. I had always thought we all had similar pains with those pains uniting us. Yet contrary to everyday aches such as toothaches, heartaches were hard to put into words and talk about. The good times had gotten stuck in our windpipes and turned into rubbish.

Silence fell as if a total power outage had come about. "Well, I'm leaving" was like a hand grenade ready to explode any moment. The silent moments between sentences were becoming ever longer, making our sitting at the same table appear to be an official duty, as if we were waiting for some deadline to expire. The stronger individual of the two of us would garner the prowess to ask for the check and leave. Being strong was important because we had been brought up under the guidance of "be strong." The one to stay longer would be the one whose love had been deeper and who would suffer more. Is that not hypocritical? Hence, I did not want to be a hypocrite, saying, "It's up to you." Those words highlighted what I had been experiencing for hours now, if not throughout our relationship.

I knew a moment of silence would occur and all the sentences uttered would rewind to the very first word. I noticed the anger in her eyes when I said, "Let's leave." I was quite aware that we still loved each other and, above all, that we both had what it took to do so.

I asked for the check. The waiter brought it with an unexpected promptness. The first sentence after a breakup goes down in history and describes everything. We stood up and put our coats on without looking at each other, like strangers.

"Can I give you a ride?" I asked her. That was an empty gesture. We were both insincere.

"No, I'm fine," she replied.

I said nothing, as if I had never given her a ride before. We just stood like that. Funny thing, it felt as if we had melted into each other. It had been her who had wanted to leave, yet now it was us who were unable to leave.

That 10-second wait was about to end when we noticed a mutual friend walking our direction. The two of us concomitantly waved at him and hugged him. He probably had never known he was loved that much. We sat down and asked for the menus again. We wanted to go through an "overtime" to our breakup.

"I didn't mean to hold you up; you were about to leave," he said, trying to be polite.

"We haven't seen each other for a long time. A cup of tea?" I said.

I knew we only had time for a cup of tea. I wanted to place a big pot of tea in the middle of the table to prolong time. We played the happy couple. I ordered a second cup of tea before even finishing the first one. I almost hand-fed our friend dessert as he was about to leave. We reminisced about an episode involving the three of us and discussed it in its minutest details. When he said, "You look great together," we both agreed with half a smile and a nod.

"No, really, you're made for each other." This time we glowed without a smile or a nod. I looked at her pointedly in an attempt to tell her that she was the one who opted "to leave."

"I should be going now. I have other friends waiting."

"Why hurry?" I meant to say, but he had already stood up and given us hugs to return the love he had been shown. We both watched as he left. We created make-believe images of ourselves. Who was going to say the first sentence, and was it going to be the last sentence?

The pesky waiter made any likelihood of reconciliation impossible by bringing the check too quickly. There was no sentence to hide behind nor time to spend in silence. We did not stand up this time. We were taken over by our damn pride, doing our best to look calm by playing with our phones. We stood up at the same time, clinging to the phones without looking at each other. I kept thinking of this absurd sentence: "We would live in a more intimate world if we managed to read each other's minds." Wouldn't it be great if she could read my mind or if I could have a speech bubble above my head saying, "I don't want you to leave"? I gathered all the totems in my inner world I had knowledge of and released them into the universe, hoping she would see them.

The waiter had already cleaned the table and was standing with us. It was time to leave. We moved at the same time and broke the silence at the same time.

"Can I give you a ride?" I said.

"No, I'm fine."

We were at a loss for a third sentence.

We were about to leave when our friend approached us in a hurry.

"I'm throwing a birthday party tomorrow. Would you like to come?"

We said "sure" at the same time. He was our savior. With a smile on our faces, we watched him return to his table, and then we turned toward each other and whispered—but not at the same time:

"Another cup of tea?"

Memories in the Air

Once the sun started sending its rays down during the summer months, you found yourself able to bake bread on your head. Heads were like baking boards with wheat flour, underarms displayed sweat stains resembling Dalmatia's coastline, and people looked like they had just walked out of a sauna. When summer tampered with its temperature settings, people felt like they were sending a message to the heat. Some were just grateful, while others blessed and blessed the inventor of the air conditioner. Some people did not talk, hoping to hold on for eternity to the air they had just inhaled. Everybody was on the roads in this beautiful country, surrounded by seas on three sides as it is. People with straw hats had filled planes, buses, and trains, hoping to find some water to put their feet in.

There was nothing you could do against the heat. It was foolish to try to defeat nature, and people were helpless to take any steps beyond setting the air conditioner lower. I was sitting in the coolest place of the house with no options whatsoever at hand. I had opened the windows and doors and invited the wind in with my whole body; however, my arm and hands were clinging to the chair's armrest. The best thing to do under such heat was to spend a few days in some cool, breezy place. The proactive and well-planned ways of my fellow citizens brought tears to my eyes, for I met with no luck finding any ticket. I continued my search, escalating my efforts to find a seat. I had even been offered a place in the cargo section, but I didn't take that seriously. Finally, I found a window seat on a bus of a company I had never heard of before.

I threw my swim trunks, toothbrush, and a few other things in my suitcase and went to the central bus station. My decision to skip the heat for a few days had created a childish excitement in my cells. One could witness a small scene of tribal migration at the bus station. It wasn't clear who was immigrating and who was emigrating. The voices wandering here and there among the buses entered one's soul as if coming from medieval darkness.

The bus arrived and opened its doors slowly, as if it had been waiting for us for two hours, rather than the other way around. Waiting was the best friend of stress; however, I was always very calm under such circumstances. I got on the bus and searched for my seat (number 37) quietly and calmly, as if I had been friends with the bus. Somebody else was sitting in the seat I was to have ownership of for the next nine hours.

"Pardon me, sir. That is my seat."

I was very polite and considerate of the age of the person. Having said those words, I had to jump over him to get to my window seat the way I would have jumped across a creek with my pants rolled up. The man in seat number 36 was past his middle age and could be considered elderly. His face looked mature, and he appeared to be grumpy. The deep, meaningful lines specific to men that age had nestled in his face, and everything he had lived through and experienced was reflected in his eyes.

The bus was almost full; the little arguments about seats had been settled, and people began asking for water. The attendant's look at those who wanted water before the trip started showed the hospitality of the bus company. The bus set in motion with a big jolt, and we were on the road.

The older gentleman next to me, whose elbow I was very careful not to touch, was staring at one spot. I tried to talk to him.

"Have a good trip."

He put an end to the conversation by replying, "Have a good trip yourself," without turning his head. Mothers teach children to be respectful and not to bother others, as well as not to talk to or eat anything from strangers. I didn't think he would give me anything anyway. Whenever I see people looking at some spot without blinking, I think they're talking to someone invisible to others.

"Would you prefer to sit by the window?"

Leaning your head against the window on long trips enables you to turn the journey into a fairy tale, like a child dreaming under a blanket. I was wondering who his heroes might be.

"Thank you, that won't be necessary," he said.

I still wanted to talk to him, but he was sitting as if his body had already left this world. The expression on his face was as harsh as the steppe we were crossing. I got a little bit closer to the window and leaned my head against the glass once he had burned all the bridges of communication. There could easily have been another seat between us.

After a while, the temperature inside became unbearable. When I had pressed the call button the fifteenth time or so, the attendant finally came over and acknowledged, "My, it's very hot over here!" He checked the fan, went over to the driver, pressed some buttons, and came back. Meanwhile, the older gentleman was still looking at the same spot.

The attendant finally said, "This fan isn't working; in fact, it's blowing hot air."

SILENCE

I blocked the fan with a plastic bag, mumbling an angry, "I see." I admired my momentary creativity as I silently made up some curses.

The only interesting aspect of the trip up to that point had been that the gentleman hadn't commented on the situation and hadn't made a big deal out of it. Sometimes the best travel companion is the one who never speaks and, if possible, sleeps without snoring. I tried to sleep accepting all that, thus recasting his silence as a lullaby. The rustle of the plastic bag over the fan made me fall asleep. My head was slowly banging against the glass.

Though my eyes knew where I was, the pictures in my mind were designing a more interesting place for me. I was building a playground in my head. I couldn't take the nine-hour trip with a malfunctioning air conditioner. I went deep into my subconscious and turned the bus window into a movie screen. I went into the opposite lane, running among the cars and trucks as if I was late getting somewhere. As I ran faster, my arms and hands got heavier with fatigue, which was uncommon for my age. I realized I was old when I saw my reflection in a car window. I went on, this time moving at a slower pace. The traffic was at a standstill, waiting for the kids who were selling tissues. I examined my face, my hands, and my looks as I was moving among cars. I greeted the young people in the cars, saluting them with age-appropriate head bows.

Faces became familiar as I walked; I started seeing the people I loved. I wanted to greet them, but they weren't old; they were actually much younger. I walked toward the girl who was eyeing me from the road's end. The girl was smiling so beautifully that the desolate land suddenly turned green. I had provided my dream with a technology that Hollywood would have envied. I looked at her with my old eyes but young heart. Yet I knew I needed to leave. I glanced at the girl, whom my heart knew but my mind couldn't remember, and collected the familiar sentences from her eyes. "We will meet again," I said, not knowing where we'd met before. Maybe we had met a long time ago and had had imaginary breaks in between our meetings.

I continued walking with my heavy body. I noticed someone hurriedly walking among the cars just like myself. I recognized his eyes as I got closer. It was my fellow passenger, wearing the same shirt and pants, but this time he wasn't old; he was in his twenties.

"How are you?"

I was surprised that he'd started the conversation.

"Let's sit over there, across the road."

We walked slowly. He showed deference for my age, letting me walk first. Making use of some memories in my subconscious, I built a bench for us to sit on by the road. As soon as we sat down, I asked a question quite atypical of me, something like, "What would you like to be if you came to this world again?" He looked away, just like the owner of seat number 36, and said, "I would like to be myself so I can love my loved ones once again."

The owner of a voice that distorted the reality of my dream nudged me, rendering both my picture and that of my fellow passenger invisible.

"Would you care for some cake?"

"Yes, please."

I was annoyed that I had been forced to return to the real life of carbohydrates by a piece of cake while catching meaningful things in the deep corners of my sleep. As the attendant gave me the cake, I made eye contact with the older gentleman. He was looking at me with a fresh smile he'd brought over from his youth. The attendant served him a cup of tea and then turned to me with a grin on his face and said, "Let me give you some water. You kept talking in your sleep. Your throat must be very dry."

As the bus moved forth on its route, we smiled and ate our cake.

Let's Meet in Stories

I had just edited my latest story and sent it to Idil, the editor of *Kafasına Göre* magazine. When you are not a writer, the weight and the responsibilities associated with the profession can permeate every story you have written. It felt like well-known writers and poets were watching me secretly from behind my sentences; after sending each story to the publisher, I felt like silently apologizing so as not to upset them, so as not to disrespect their efforts and their troubles.

All that noise would be replaced with silence after I had completed and sent the stories. I would enjoy silence for a while, then I would try to sow new seeds involving new sentences as soon as my inner field turned arid. I switched the kettle on. I was going to have a cup of pleasure tea, delighted by the idea of having submitted my story on time, when I received a return message from Idil in my email.

Hello,

I've enjoyed reading your story, but I wish you had made the joke a little earlier. We've just finished editing the magazine's pages. There's no time left for a new design. :(

I didn't get what she was talking about. I love to joke, but one shouldn't joke when writing, when ensuring their livelihood. I immediately called her and asked what joke she was referring to in her email. She answered with her ever-ready laughter and told me about the joke. I asked the same question after I listened to her:

"Are you kidding?"

"What?!?"

I had to learn the truth by going back and forth with this joke like in a tennis game. It was a story that I had long had in my mind, yet had never told anyone about. One of the stories submitted in the reader's corner of the magazine was identical to my story. I understood what she meant when I started reading that story. If it was meant as a joke, it surely targeted me. The sender had an email address only . . .

I tried to find a familiar face among hundreds of accounts and images registered to Feride Yildirim. The fact that she had sent her story before me made me a plagiarist, and I didn't want to fall victim to a silly joke. I didn't want to experience modern human paranoia thinking that my computer may have been hacked. There are no unspoken words under the sun, yet how could I have written the exact same story as someone I didn't know and had never seen in my life?

I put aside my astonishment and started going through the white pages of my memory. I wondered if I had been influenced by some story by one of my favorite writers. We might both have loved the same story and stored it in our subconscious. This could have happened except the story I had written was about me. My topic was not relevant to great writers, poets, and storytellers. Interestingly, I had written the story from a male's point of view, and she had written it from a female's point of view. A man remembers a picture of an island he saw in his childhood. He sees the island in his dreams, wakes up in a sweat, buys a plane ticket that very moment, and goes to the island without taking anything with him. He meets a woman on that island. They fall in love . . .

The story about going to the island, the sentences describing that place were the very same in the two stories. It was like the meeting point of our imaginary worlds. It was possible to meet in stories if the famous writers, who were hidden behind their sentences, allowed it. I took a sip of my cold tea and started typing an email:

Hello,

I would like you to read the attached story. Your submission of your story before mine might make you think I am mocking you. This may very well be a mere coincidence, but I would like you to know that this story is extremely dear to me. I don't expect you to reply. I just wanted to make you aware.

All the best to you.

After sending the email, I wondered who this person was. My email was a bit cold, but her response would enable me to know her—the person hiding behind the sentences. The main point behind the story I had written was pursuit of a feeling. When attempts were made to describe it and render it visible, it appeared fragile enough to wither in the swamp of one's mind. I'm not saying this to add literary meaning to the story; I am just trying to emphasize that people who feel and think like us do exist. Even if we believe we are alone in the universe, stories, sentences—and even words—may make us experience the same feelings and unite us. It must be something similar to what twins go through.

One of my other stories did get published in the magazine. The "twinning stories" did not. Idil and Yasin still thought that I was joking and had written both stories. I did not wish to talk about it anymore. In the long run, it was a private matter and shouldn't become the subject of a trivial conversation. I erased the island story from my computer, from my memory, and from my emotions. I tried to pretend that I had never written such a story.

***

The literary magazine *Kafasına Göre* was published bimonthly, and the due date for my new story was approaching fast. While thinking what to write about, my mind kept going back to the island story. It appeared to be unfinished. There was something incomplete about it, a feeling of something missing. It affected my wording and made itself visible whenever new venues were not properly established but were just roaming my mind. I chose the topic of lack of belief in oneself for my new story, which meant new emotions and venues. I finished and sent it in great haste. Following that, as usual, I had a cup of tea, delighted that I had sent in a new story.

I surrendered to the pleasure of sleeping on the couch. I fell asleep softly. The potful of tea I had drunk caused my stomach to bloat, a physical condition just suitable for sleep. I walked along that thin line between sleep and wake, not knowing which of them to fall for and submitting to silence. I walked at a slow pace, and each step took me closer to falling asleep. I could feel the water rising from my feet to my ankles. I was in the sea, walking toward its deep end and trying to figure out how to take each next step. The pebbles hurting my feet and the seaweed I felt in my toes helped me understand where I was.

As soon as I looked up, I knew I was on the same island. The sun was about to set—or maybe it had just risen. The time of day had little importance; it was good to be in the water. In my story, I had been to the island before, had taken a long flight, and had fallen in love. My words had created sentences, and my sentences had created the invisible subtleties of the woman I'd fallen in love with. Would I be able to see and remember the woman in my story again?

It wasn't a desert island. People were swimming, jumping off the pier, having lunch and laughing, gazing at the sun and the clouds. Everybody was having a good time; a picture surfaced that compelled reality. Everyone around me seemed to be rehearsing the world I was dreaming about. I started scrutinizing the crowd, looking for the woman I had fallen in love with amid the people laughing and having fun.

My sleep on the couch was disturbed by a deep sigh. My curved body was numb, and my ankles felt wet. I forced myself up and took a shower; being under the water felt good on my numb body. I realized that the island story was not only going to roam in my head, but also visit me in my dreams. I went back to the couch and sat down again. While thinking about how to word the rest of the story, an email message caught my attention.

> Hello,
>
> I am Feride Yildirim. I've read in amazement the story you sent. If you want to read the rest of the story I've written, see the attachment.
>
> Best.

"I was in the sea. I was looking around as if waiting for something. I noticed a man amid the people laughing and having fun, looking down at the water. He was obviously not familiar with the island. He was careful about his steps. The beauty of the place was giving his soul courage, and he wanted to take bigger steps. As I got closer, I knew who he was. The man I'd fallen in love with had come back to the island."

It's Mellow!

"Mellow!"

"Purr..."

He was sitting in the best spot of the sofa, looking at me with an uncanny expression without lifting his head. At such a moment, he would add meaning to our unique relationship with his tabby body. He would understand what I was about to say and made his voice heard—one that meant the same in all languages—with a barely perceptible yawn. He would not only look at me with those glowing eyes without lifting his head but would also foresee what I was about to say.

"Purr..."

I rehearsed which comma I would breathe during the process of connecting my words into my sentences.

"I have a girlfriend."

"Purr..."

"It's kind of new. I mean, it's not been going on for long."

He lifted his head, stretched his body, and appeared to be saying, "Go on..."

"Well, we are in love and have decided to live together."

This time he didn't lift his head; he turned his back on me and lifted his tail.

"She's going to move in with..."

His purring intensified, and he tucked his head under the pillow. I could tell he didn't want to hear the rest by the wag of his tail.

"Well..."

He would have to share his sofa and his desk with another person; to be more precise, his house would be ruined.

"Well, she has a cat too."

He left the room without giving me the chance to finish.

"Meow..."

A week later my girlfriend and Linda, her white Angora cat with blue eyes, moved in. I could tell from her posture, the symmetrical spread of her fur, and the calmness in her blue eyes that she hadn't had a difficult life. She displayed the cuteness of female cats, and she was making it clear that she meant to be the new house pet. Mellow occupied the best spot on the sofa as if indicating that the house was his. He didn't move or greet them by wagging his tail. Basically, he showed that he was no hospitable cat. Linda seemed like a well-behaved cat. She did her best to get used to my house even though she came from a much larger house and was used to better conditions. She strove to gracefully overshadow Mellow's rude behavior by means of her cuteness and soft fur.

My girlfriend brought in her second suitcase, then the third. We had a strong tie with the suitcase coefficient, which lifted her from the rank of guest to that of host, and she soon became a host rather than a guest. Naturally, Linda left her scent in all the places she liked and gradually became the new homeowner. As the number of suitcases increased, Mellow and I started looking at each other. I could hear the cuss words he was silently producing. I could understand those from the undertones in his purr. I was afraid to show any interest in Linda. I allowed myself that only behind closed doors.

Our home life, now involving two boys and two girls, went on calmly and cussing laden. I loved my girlfriend; having her in my home and in my bed made me very happy. Our precious, sweet, and affectionate words would hit the walls and bounce back onto Mellow's lap, undergo processing there, and get back to me with an irritated cuss. I was fine, barring Mellow's grudges. I was in nice relationship, and I knew enough about life not to question things that were going well.

The breakfasts, the long chats during tea time, and frequent visits by friends kept our relationship warm. Whenever silence befell the house, something inside me would immediately ignite like dried grass. When there's no longer talking and sharing between a couple, silence follows, which can bring about a fire to burn down a forest. I ran away from silence and sank myself into a crowd of noises. We had guests over every day; we found solace in noise and conversations with friends.

Mellow started not talking to me during the second month of my relationship. I was aware that he meant to tell me something, for he knew me better than I knew myself. As the number of guests decreased, the relationship started to sour. The scary inner screams that our silence created showed in our eyes. Silence was on the rise, even though we knew we had a lot to talk about and a lot to share. Mellow and Linda started finding each other in that silence. The levels of their cuteness were increasing. We could sense the first murmurs of great love. Chatting with our friends no longer solved our spats. The phones in our palms had come to be our saviors. An invisible wall had risen between us, even though we shared the same sofa. There were holes in the walls of our relationship, a relationship that had shrunk to the size of a hand.

A sound bomb, stuck in the silence, exploded in my heart first, only to spread all over my body and leave a bitter taste in my mouth. My girlfriend was putting together sentences that did not have verbs and were not reaching my heart. She eventually pulled the pin of her last sentence and handed it to me:

"I'm leaving."

She took Linda and left. The suitcases that had come in installments were all gone at once. Mellow was unhappy about Linda's departure and started shaming me with his looks.

"Do you even know what love is?" said the cat.

"Of course I do."

"I don't think so! You don't. You've ruined my happiness too."

"You always put yourself first."

"You think so! You are wrong about cats!"

I was sitting in the worst spot of the sofa and talking to my cat. Was I freaking out, or did the buzzing words make me lose my mind?

Three months went by. My sour relationship with Mellow had gotten a little sweeter. At least I would get a "good morning" now. There still were times when we both became quite grumpy though; before going to bed, we put all the tiredness of the day on our faces.

Mellow's eyes were half-open; my annoyance was about to intertwine with sleep when we heard a scratch at the door. The sound woke us both and took us to the door. It was Linda. She'd run away from home and had followed the scents, had followed her heart.

"Purr... purr..."

Only the three of us were able to understand what Linda had said:

"It's Mellow..."

About the author

Engin Akyürek was born in 1981 in Ankara, Turkey. He graduated from the University of Ankara with a bachelor's degree in history. He has starred in many movies and TV series since 2004. He continues to express himself by writing short stories in *Kafasına Göre* literary magazine.

Printed in the USA
CPSIA information can be obtained
at www.ICGtesting.com
LVHW011734220124
769643LV00056B/1748